"Geneva. How long has it been?"

What game was he playing? "You know as well as I do how long."

Michael looked steady and thoughtful, but that didn't fool her. His jaw muscle tightening was a clue.

"Oh, you mean the wedding," he said. "The one where you left me at the altar."

She winced. How simple he made it sound. But it hadn't been simple, and seeing him again dredged up all the painful feelings that had compelled her to leave him that day.

Oh, he'd been *willing* to go through with the wedding—because he'd given his word. But Geneva had wanted more than just willing. She wanted love—the head-over-heels kind. The kind that could make a marriage work.

The kind this man couldn't give her.

Dear Reader,

I live in Las Vegas, which proclaims itself the most exciting city on the planet. Certainly it's one of the fastest growing, and the high-rise development concept has taken hold here in a big way. It's also the wedding capital of the world.

This seemed an appropriate backdrop for the story of a rich developer who falls in love at first sight and the woman who calls off their wedding for fear of making a mistake. In *Winning Back His Bride* Michael Sullivan falls all over again for Geneva Porter as they both realize theirs is the kind of love that will make a marriage last.

I hope you enjoy their story.

All the best,

Teresa Southwick

Winning
Back His
Bride

TERESA
SOUTHWICK

SILHOUETTE *Romance*®

Published by Silhouette Books

America's Publisher of Contemporary Romance

 SILHOUETTE BOOKS

ISBN-13: 978-0-373-19831-3
ISBN-10:   0-373-19831-0

WINNING BACK HIS BRIDE

First North American Publication 2006

Visit Silhouette Books at www.eHarlequin.com

Printed in U.S.A.

TERESA SOUTHWICK

is delighted to be living out her lifelong dream of writing for Silhouette Romance and Silhouette Special Edition. She lives in Las Vegas, where she's hard at work on her next romance novel.

"Las Vegas is renowned as the wedding capital of the world, so when I decided to set this book here, I knew a wedding would figure prominently. And what if that wedding was one that didn't happen? This was the core idea behind this book. I live in Las Vegas, and find it really is the most exciting city on the planet."

Look out for Teresa Southwick's next story,
CRAZY ABOUT THE BOSS #3924
On-sale in December from Harlequin Romance®

This story is part of an exciting new continuity,
THE BRIDES OF BELLA LUCIA
A family torn apart by secrets, reunited by marriage

This month, don't miss
THE REBEL PRINCE
by Raye Morgan #3912

Only from Harlequin Romance®!

To Stacy Boyd,
an editor with the perfect blend of
efficiency, creativity and support.
You're the best!

CHAPTER ONE

PICTURE him naked.

Geneva Porter was familiar with the technique public speakers used to calm nerves, but it wouldn't work for her. This wasn't public. She wasn't speaking. And she'd already seen Michael Sullivan naked.

However hot the memory, seeing the sexy Mr. Sullivan without his clothes was partially responsible for the disastrous series of events that had landed her right here, right now—waiting to see him and find out if she was Las Vegas's latest events planner without a job.

Unemployment would be bad. Seeing Michael Sullivan again... It was going to be very bad.

But he was her boss as of a week ago when his deal to buy this hotel finalized. One by one he'd met with the existing managers. Now it was her turn. Time to get it over with and brazen out their first meeting since... Well, since she'd last seen him. On the bad scale, that time had been off the chart.

Taking a deep breath wouldn't help but she took one anyway as she knocked sharply on his door and let herself in. It was a spacious corner office with two sets of floor-to-ceiling windows, giving him two different and fabulous views of the Las Vegas Strip, Bellagio on one side, Caesar's Palace on the other. Michael was sitting behind his desk oozing power and charisma.

"Hello, Michael." One look into his dark eyes dropped her stomach like the Insanity ride on top of the Stratosphere. Her heart pounded and her hands shook. "You look great."

How stupid did that sound? This was worse than bad.

She'd met him over a year ago when he'd started the process of buying this property. He hadn't changed a bit. He looked just as handsome, with his dark hair and a face that was all lean angles. But it was his smile that she'd fallen in love with and she wasn't seeing it now.

"Geneva." His eyes narrowed and a muscle jumped in his jaw. "How long has it been?"

What game was he playing? "You know as well as I do how long."

He looked steady and thoughtful but that didn't fool her. The jaw muscle tightening again was a clue.

"Oh. You mean the wedding," he said.

"Of course that's what I mean."

"The one where you left me at the altar."

She winced. How simple he made it sound. How easily he said the words. But it hadn't been simple or easy and seeing him again dredged up all the painful feelings that had compelled her to leave him that day. She feared making a mistake, a mistake too much like her parents had made by marrying each other. Feared that Michael had never loved her, that he'd proposed only because she'd been pregnant with his child, a baby she'd miscarried in the first trimester.

He'd been *willing* to go through with the wedding—because he'd given his word. But, Geneva wanted more than just willing. She wanted love—the head-over-heels kind. The only kind that could fill the emptiness in her soul for the baby she'd lost. The only kind that would make a marriage work.

Brushing nonexistent lint from the skirt of her black suit, she said, "About the wedding—"

He held up a hand to stop her. "That's not why I called you in."

"But it's why you're going to fire me."

One dark eyebrow rose. "Why would I do that?"

She badly wanted to say "duh." Instead she put as much sass as possible into the look she shot him. "Maybe *because* I left you at the altar?"

"That was a year ago."

As if she didn't know. "So you're over it?"

"Of course."

Of course? Just like that? So now she had new and different feelings yet to be identified. She didn't want him to brood over her. She hadn't wanted to hurt him in the first place. But he was dismissing her like an afterthought. She should be relieved. If she worked hard enough, maybe she could pull it off.

"Good," she said, nodding. "I guess that explains why you went ahead with the hotel deal."

"It's business," he snapped.

"It's Vegas," she countered. "Mergers and acquisitions are announced every other week. A gazillion things have to fall into place before anyone signs on the dotted line. Deals fall apart all the time."

"You thought I'd back out because of you?" he asked. His voice could've frozen a glass of water in the middle of July.

"Wouldn't it have been easier?"

"I don't take the easy way out." His gaze locked on hers and clearly said—not like some people. "And I'm getting the feeling you don't want to work for me."

Probably because she didn't. Not if she had to see him regularly. "I don't have a choice. It's called a contract. Although as the new owner of this hotel, you can terminate it."

"Why would I do that?"

"Because you're angry and want revenge. What happened between us was very public and—"

"Very over," he interrupted. "It didn't change my mind about the deal. I wanted this hotel for the adjacent land."

And he'd only wanted her for the baby. That still hurt deeply. "I see."

His gaze narrowed. "Are you wondering if I still have personal feelings for you?"

"I'm wondering if your personal feelings are about getting even with me," she said, putting a finer point on it.

"I'd be lying if I said the thought hadn't crossed my mind. I'm not a turn-the-other-cheek kind of guy."

No. He was a man-of-action kind of guy. They'd barely been introduced when he swept her off her feet. After all this time apart, just a few minutes with him showed her she was still vulnerable to the Michael Sullivan brand of charm. And he wasn't being charming.

Still standing in front of his desk, she squared her shoulders and linked her fingers together, refusing to let him see that her hands were shaking. "Did you call me in to ask for my resignation?"

"I called you in because you're the hotel events planner." Something dangerous flared in his eyes. "I want you to plan an event." He held out his hand, indicating the chairs in front of his desk. "Why don't you sit down?"

Did she have a choice? She needed this job. She had a year left on her contract. If she walked, he could sue her for breach of contract and she had no doubt he would—because he wasn't a turn-the-other-cheek kind of guy. Defending herself against a lawsuit could get expensive and ruin the professional reputation she'd been working so hard to build in Las Vegas. On top of that, she'd refinanced her condo and borrowed against the equity to pay Michael back for the wedding.

"Okay." Since she couldn't walk out, she sat.

"As you know, I have real estate and hotels in the east, and this is my second hotel in Las Vegas."

"Yes."

He folded his hands and rested them on his glass and chrome desk as he leaned forward. "I'm planning a luxury high-rise on the land that adjoins this hotel. It's a fairly new concept to Las Vegas and will give the Vegas Valley its vertical identity. The tallest residential super tower west of the Mississippi will also make this a flagship property for the upscale Sullivan brand's global footprint."

"Very ambitious."

"I'm an ambitious man. This is the only city in the world that reinvents itself every day. And now it's my city with all its possibilities—and risks."

She knew all about risk. She'd found out she wasn't a risk-taker but that hadn't saved her from regrets. With an effort, she pulled her thoughts back to what he was saying.

Dark intensity sizzled in his eyes. "It's a good location, with spectacular views of the lights on The Strip and close to downtown restaurants, shows and high-end shopping."

"Sounds like New York west."

"That's the plan. But we need to hit the ground running at the grand opening."

"Did you have any thoughts about what tone you want to set at the sales release?" She was the planner, but it was his event.

He nodded. "Glitzy, in a three-ring circus kind of way. The biggest dog and pony show you can possibly pull off."

"I can pull off whatever you want."

He didn't respond, but the muscle in his jaw jerked, and she wondered if he was thinking about the day she'd walked away. She shouldn't still care what he thought, but he was her boss and all she had was her job. So she'd best start doing it and focus on the here and now instead of on the past.

She sat up straighter and met his gaze. "Glitz would include Hollywood A-listers. Entertainment personalities with a lot of money to spend and wealthy noncelebrities. It should be invitation only, and we send them out to everyone you know or ever hope to know."

"You're the expert."

Did he really think that? Or was he setting her up for a fall? "Then I'll brainstorm some promotion and giveaway ideas. Nothing brings people out like a spectacle and freebies. Did you have a theme in mind?" she asked.

"Again, that's your field of expertise."

"Sullivan Towers, the sky's the limit," she said off the top of her head. "Or 'Living the High Life.'"

"Not bad." His dark eyes gleamed with reluctant approval.

Geneva felt the power of that unwilling positive reaction deep down inside, pressing against a place she'd closed off a year ago. It was a Pandora's box of feelings: messy, confusing, disturbing and embarrassing.

Yes, she'd called off the wedding. Her mistake had been in waiting until just before saying "I do." But until that moment, she'd tried to convince herself that Michael actually loved her. If she'd gone through with the ceremony knowing he didn't, she'd have been destroyed. And so would he. But he'd never given her the chance to explain that she'd done him a favor.

"So are we finished?" she asked.

"For now."

Very bad didn't begin to describe this meeting. And he would know how she felt unless she got out of here now.

"I'll work up a proposal." She stood. "But before I get started, Michael, I need an answer to my question."

"Which one?" he asked, standing too.

She looked way up at him, six feet of solid muscle and sophisticated suave sex appeal. Her insides quivered with memories of the short time he'd been hers. Then the memories became a fist squeezing her heart, making it difficult to draw in air.

"Do you intend to terminate my contract because of what happened between us?"

He settled his hands on lean hips. "Didn't we just have a meeting about an event I expect you to plan?"

"I got that. But are you going to change your mind? We'll have to work closely together and I wouldn't blame you if you couldn't work with me at all." If he simply let her out of her contract, it would be the clean break she needed to avoid this emotional free-for-all *and* maintain her professional reputation.

"That would imply I hadn't forgiven you."

"Have you?"

Michael folded his arms over his impressive chest and smiled his pretty smile, the one that always crumbled her defenses like stick houses in a stiff breeze. "I always say—forgive your enemies. It messes with their heads."

That was nothing new. For the last year thoughts of him had messed with her head even when she hadn't seen him. Now he was back in her life and that meant he could mess with her heart unless she figured out a way to Michael-proof it.

"Geneva. I need—"

Need? The word stopped Michael. He didn't need, not from her. He wouldn't let himself need anything from her. At least not personally. Professional needs were different.

"We have to talk."

Michael watched her back stiffen and braced himself. He thought he'd done that a week ago, before seeing her again. He'd thought he'd been prepared for eyes so big, so green he could fall into them. For the thick, shiny brown hair that made him want to bury his fingers in the silken strands. For the deep dimples that could drop a man to his knees when she smiled and the body that could tempt him to throw caution to the wind.

He'd thought wrong.

It had been a year, for God's sake, and when she'd walked into his office he'd wanted to terminate her contract on the spot. The problem was, he was still putting together the project's financing. His past with Geneva was no secret, and firing her could be a disaster. Perception was everything. If he couldn't handle having an old girlfriend around, how was he going to deal with the stress of a billion-dollar development?

Or worse, it could look like he was reacting emotionally, which would fuel rumors that he couldn't manage the company with a steady hand and a clear head. None of it was a big deal, but he'd seen the stock market rise and fall on less. Any hint of weakness could be enough to trigger investor doubt. Without investors, the project would be dead in the water.

That was unacceptable. He was stuck with her, and he'd realized it when he'd decided to go forward with the deal. But he'd had a year to prepare himself. It should have been enough.

He'd expected to feel nothing and hadn't been ready for the grinding knot of need at his first glimpse of Geneva. He wouldn't make the same mistake.

He'd deliberately waited a week to see her again, giving her time to squirm and wonder what he was up to. The meeting of his operations team had just ended. He hadn't missed the fact that Geneva sat in the chair closest to the door—and farthest from him.

So what else was new? She'd left him at the altar. Like an idiot, he'd actually thought about going after her. Before making a fool of himself he realized there was nothing to talk about. She'd said she couldn't marry him. End of story.

As she walked toward him now, his gaze settled on her mouth and a jolt of awareness arced through him. End of attraction? Not so much.

She stopped two feet away from him, at the head of the long, mahogany conference table. "Yes?"

"Something's come up," he said.

"Don't tell me. You changed your mind."

"About?"

"Firing me." She lowered her voice and glanced over her shoulder at the group of executives milling around talking. Then she met his gaze again. "You wanted more witnesses when you made the announcement."

"And why would I want that?" He was irritated when he caught himself staring at her mouth again.

"An eye for an eye."

"You still think I'm after revenge."

"A natural assumption considering you once told me your philosophy. And not the one about forgiving your enemies."

She shrugged and tried to look as if she didn't give a damn. It didn't work. One of the things he'd instantly liked about her was that everything she was thinking showed on her face. She couldn't hide what she was feeling. Then she'd proven him wrong by blindsiding him the day he'd planned to make her his. And it *had* been very public. Especially for a man who didn't like getting blindsided at all.

The day she'd left him at the altar had been the second worst day of his life. It was only topped by the day he'd found out his parents were killed in a plane crash.

He forced the thoughts away and struggled to focus. "I have another philosophy?"

"Don't get mad. Get even," she reminded him. "And stay on top."

"Ah." He nodded. "That one."

Getting mad didn't help. He'd tried that first. He'd also considered backing out of the hotel deal after she'd backed out of their wedding. But he refused to let her win. He also couldn't fire her. Getting even? The thought held some appeal.

"So am I canned?" she asked.

"No."

"Then what did you want to talk to me about?" she asked guardedly.

"Teri is getting married."

"Please convey my congratulations to your sister."

"You can do it yourself. You're going to plan the engagement party and wedding."

She stared at him for several moments. "Isn't this where you say 'gotcha?'"

"I couldn't be more serious."

She shook her head in disbelief. "Your sister could elevate grudge-holding to an art form. The Teri Sullivan I know would take her vows at city hall and meet at Fatburger for the reception before letting the same woman who left her brother at the altar plan her wedding."

"Maybe. But Teri still wants you."

Struggling for indifference, Michael slid his hands into his pockets. How the hell could *he* still want her after all this time? After what she'd done? But he knew. He'd never quite been able to *stop* wanting her. Or stop missing the feel of her in his arms at night. And he was having trouble getting the "hands off" message from his brain to the appropriate body parts. At least he could explain that. It was a purely physical reaction to a strikingly beautiful woman.

Everything else was more complicated. He'd told himself it was just business, but two meetings with Geneva had shown him that seeing her every day would be an unexpected complication. He didn't like complications.

But sometimes to get the job done you had to piss people off, even if that person was yourself. Success didn't come without a price and he was determined that the cost wouldn't be more than he could pay.

Geneva shook her head. "I don't understand."

"My sister's a team player."

Questions simmered in her eyes. "And, pray tell, why is her wedding a team event?"

"Let's call it one part of the marketing strategy. A celebrity wedding will generate media attention and get the word out to our target buyer. I paid the idea guys a lot of money for their expertise and it would take a special kind of stupid to ignore them."

"What aren't you telling me, Michael?"

If he didn't know better, he'd think that was concern in her eyes. But he did know better. "I need to secure the rest of the financing for Sullivan Towers. We have enough to break ground and build a shell, but not to finish. That would make it a very public failure. Been there. Done that. Don't want to go there again."

She caught the corner of her top lip between her teeth. "If you're talking about the wedding, I had reasons for calling it off—"

"It's not about you." He wouldn't let it be. And he didn't want to hear her excuses now any more than he had then. Her actions had told him everything he needed to know. "That's ancient history."

"But it was my public failure, not yours."

"Yes, and your failure will help me get my financing. The press will dig into everything about Teri and me *and* you. They write about everything we Sullivans do and the public reads it."

"I remember," she said.

"The only thing that generates more publicity than a high profile wedding is one that *doesn't* happen." Their fiasco had fueled a reporter feeding frenzy. "The day you walked out we were the lead story on the news, beating out the president's summit on the global economy."

"Yeah. For months afterward they hounded me for a comment."

Which she'd stubbornly declined to make. He respected her discretion even though he didn't want to respect anything about her. "I got the same treatment. So imagine a Sullivan business venture combined with a Sullivan wedding... Picture the headlines—millionaire developer gains luxury highrise and loses sister to matrimony. Wedding to be planned by his runaway bride. The perfect storm of publicity."

"I see your point," she said.

"I thought you would."

"But I can't do it." She folded her arms beneath her breasts.

He couldn't stop himself from noticing the interesting things the movement did to her curves and memories of soft skin and twisted sheets jumped into his mind. He forced himself to look away. When he glanced around the room, he saw that it was empty except for him and Geneva. Where had everyone gone? More to the point—when had they gone and why hadn't he noticed? Damn it.

Clearly she didn't want to be here. Tough. He didn't want to be here, either, let alone asking her to do anything more than her job required. But he and Teri were determined to make Sullivan Towers a success and that meant doing the hard stuff.

His sister had no qualms about working with Geneva. Her reservations had been for him. But he'd assured her that he had no leftover feelings. It had been a year and Geneva didn't matter. If they could use public failure and turn it into a success, he'd lead the way.

She shook her head. "I'm sorry, Michael. I just don't want to cause you problems."

"That's ironic coming from you," he snapped.

Something flashed in her eyes, but she didn't respond.

"Teri is the only family I have left. If you choose to believe anything, believe this—I wouldn't do anything to hurt her."

He'd been eighteen and Teri just ten when their parents died. But they'd pulled together and moved forward. And that's the way they would make this project an unqualified success.

Geneva worried her lip between her teeth as she

studied him. "Michael, clearly this has been in the works for a while. Why didn't you mention this to me that day in your office?"

He shrugged. "I had other things on my mind."

No way would he tell her that seeing her again and acting as if he felt nothing had taken all of his concentration. Everything else had slipped his mind.

He ran his fingers through his hair. "The bottom line is that I need to presell forty percent of the high-rise units to secure the last of the financing before we break ground. We'll leave no stone unturned and take advantage of the press, publicity and media exposure wherever we can find it. You're part of that whether you like it or not."

"And if I refuse you'll fire me?"

"That's not the kind of publicity I'm after." Was she hoping he'd let her go? Put distance between them? Bailing out was what she did best, but he wouldn't let her get away with it this time. The project was the highest profile development he'd ever done and he was dedicating it to his parents. He'd do whatever was necessary to make it happen, including using her. "Look at it this way. You owe me, Geneva."

She stared at him for several moments, doubts swirling in her eyes. The uncertainty was still there when she nodded and said, "Okay."

"Okay what?"

"Maybe there really is something I can do to help

you get what you want and make up for what I did. I'm willing to take a chance. Because, God knows you have your faults, Michael. A good many of them. As do I. But you'd never do anything to hurt your sister. Not even for business."

That was true. If Teri had the slightest doubt about this aspect of the marketing plan, he'd find another angle for the media attention.

"Then we have a deal."

"We do. And for now I'll assume you're not trying to lull me into a false sense of security, then—" She drew her hand across her neck, miming slitting her throat.

Get her? A shaft of heat lasered through him and again he did his best to ignore it. He straightened and looked down at her. "To still be angry enough to get even with you over what happened a year ago requires a great deal of energy and passion. I've focused both on opening Sullivan Towers."

"You've made that abundantly clear."

"Good." And speaking of passion, it was time to put his back to work before he forgot to forget and remembered to remember everything about her. He walked toward the door and said, "I'll be in touch."

Touch.

Like the exquisite sensation of her bare skin beneath his hands, her lips responding to his own. Those memories gave a whole new meaning to the words *I'll be in touch.*

His intense reaction irritated the hell out of him. He didn't want to want her, but that made no difference to his testosterone. And with so much at stake, he couldn't afford any weakness.

He didn't have to like the idea of working with her, but he wouldn't let her become a distraction. Since he didn't have a choice, he'd make the most of a bad situation. He'd make sure his sister had the best and if that meant hiring Geneva as the wedding planner and watching her every step of the way, he'd do it. That would never make up for Teri not having her father and mother there to give her away, but Michael intended to create a wedding day she would never forget. And he wasn't above using the situation to his advantage. Since a year without Geneva hadn't taken the edge off his attraction, perhaps overexposure would do the trick. Might be just what he needed to get her out of his system.

The best part was that she wouldn't like it.

CHAPTER TWO

"HI, TERI." Geneva cradled the phone between her ear and shoulder, then swiveled her office chair around to look out the window. "Thanks for calling me back."

She still couldn't believe she'd actually agreed to plan this wedding. Although *agreed* was stretching reality. She'd been backed into a corner—damned if she did, damned if she didn't. Refusing would have the same results as walking out—breach of contract and goodbye career. Still, Michael had all but said this would help him and somehow that made it different. The man she remembered hadn't needed her. Which made her wonder if Michael had something up his sleeve besides a very muscular arm.

"Your message said you wanted to discuss wedding plans." Teri Sullivan's voice was cool, but that was to be expected.

Michael's sister was a beautiful brunette, tall, slim, dark-eyed. Her fiancé, Geneva had learned, was

Michael's best friend Dexter Smith, a good-looking geek and chief numbers cruncher for Sullivan, Inc. They'd looked especially spectacular a year ago in their maid of honor and best man ensembles. And both of them loved Michael. Working with them wouldn't be easy. Which might be what Michael wanted. Whoever said payback was a bitch hadn't exaggerated.

Geneva let out a long breath. "I wanted to talk to you because we have to start making decisions."

"Like what?"

"For starters, you should be shopping for a dress. I can recommend some designers who will bring sketches to you."

"That would be great."

"Next on the list would be the location. We need to find a place you love that can also accommodate your guest list."

Big sigh on the other end of the phone. "I don't have time for that."

Teri worked with Dex in the financial end of the corporation and chances were good that the two were deeply involved in securing the necessary funding for Sullivan Towers.

"If you'd like, I can look and gather information, then report back to you."

"Again, great."

"Okay. Good. I'll take care of all the details. I want to assure you that the wedding will be perfect."

"I have no doubt." There was steel and sarcasm in her voice. "You owe Michael."

He'd told Geneva the same thing. And he was right. "I'm aware of the debt."

"I'm not talking financially," Teri added. "Dex told me about the check you sent to reimburse my brother for the wedding costs. What's that about?"

"It was the right thing." Michael knew all about doing the right thing. She swiveled around, saw Michael standing in the doorway and dropped the phone. "Good grief."

"What's the right thing?" he asked.

"That would be you wearing a bell around your neck," she said as she repositioned the receiver.

"For the wedding?" Teri sounded surprised.

"No. The fashion police would be all over that. I was talking to your brother. He sneaked up on me."

And it was becoming an annoying habit. Every day he dropped in and lounged in her doorway—early morning, just before quitting time, or, like now, lunchtime when her assistant Chloe was out of the office. Probably just as well. Chloe thought Geneva needed therapy for dumping such a hottie. Geneva agreed that she needed her head examined. The childhood from hell tended to do that to a girl.

"Tell him hi for me." Teri's tone was noticeably warmer and it was hard to tell whether that was about what she'd learned from Dex or for her brother.

"Teri says hi." She watched him nod, then forced

herself to ignore him, which wasn't easy, what with her pulse going a mile a minute. "Okay, here's the plan. I'll do some research on chapels, then get back to you."

"Okay. Gotta go."

"Bye," she said as the line went dead, and wished she could say the same for her hormones. But they had a mind of their own and disobeyed orders every time she saw Michael. How she wished he would stay away.

"To what do I owe the pleasure?" she asked.

It was better phrasing than, "What the heck are you doing here," which had been on the tip of her tongue.

He held up a bag. "I brought you a sandwich."

"Why?" That sounded suspicious and ungrateful, but from her point of view perfectly appropriate.

"Because it's time for lunch."

Why didn't he just go away and quit bugging her? "How do you know I don't have a stash of candy in my desk drawer?"

He let his gaze wander over her bare arms and settle on her breasts. If she wasn't sitting at her desk she just knew he'd have dragged that look all the way to her ankles and toes. The thought made her shiver.

"I don't think so." He scanned her desk, searching for a spot to set the bag. "Where do you want this?"

Geneva's workspace was always cluttered. If anything was put away, she couldn't find what she needed when she needed it. Her desk was teak and glass, although she couldn't prove it at the moment. But she knew it was there somewhere.

She eyed the bag suspiciously. "If it's going to blow up, you can chuck it down the hallway."

"Turkey and tomato isn't explosive." He stared down at her, his expression infuriatingly unreadable. "You have to let the whole retaliation thing go."

"No, I don't." She moved a stack of papers and he set down the bag. "I can hang onto my paranoia just as long as I want."

Retribution could come at any time, in any form. Like just before Sullivan Towers grand opening where she could publicly take the blame if the event tanked. That would seriously undermine her reputation and in her line of work that was everything. But so far, Michael only showed up in her office every day, just long enough to stir her up. Advance and retreat. To her that spelled guerrilla warfare. Only, instead of camouflage, he wore gray slacks, a white shirt and a pewter and black striped tie. As commandos went, he sure knew how to dress.

"Paranoia it is then." He stared at her desk, probably looking for an uncluttered place to lean against.

For once Geneva was grateful to her inner slob. It kept him out of her space and set up a perimeter. "Thanks for the sandwich," she said, trying to be gracious.

"You're welcome." He sat in one of the chrome and tweed upholstered chairs in front of her. "So, you were talking to Teri. How are the wedding plans coming?"

"Oh." She shrugged. "You know."

"Actually I don't know."

She leaned back in her chair and studied his face, but his expression was hooded. "There's not much to tell. Everything is preliminary at the moment."

He rested his elbows on his knees and linked his fingers. "Tell me about the preliminaries."

"It's all very vague. I've got threads here and there. When I pull them into some kind of cohesive plan, I'd be happy to update you."

"Actually I'm not asking for a favor. It's your job to keep me informed every step of the way."

She stared at him. "Define every step."

What he was proposing would mean seeing him a lot more than she'd thought. After leaving her wedding, she'd kept two phones and a pager at her fingertips in case he wanted to talk to her. She'd waited and hoped for the opportunity to explain, but he'd never contacted her. He'd just let her go. She'd thought he would fight harder, but he hadn't fought for her at all. Now he wanted to be joined at the hip?

His gaze captured hers. "Every step means every single decision. If you pick out flowers, I want to know what color the pistils are."

"You're micromanaging."

"You bet I am." His voice lowered dangerously. "Everything is going to get media attention. It's got to be perfect. Millions of dollars are riding on it. I've got a lot at stake and I need to know I can depend on you."

The look in his eyes, the tone in his voice, both added up to one thing and it wasn't about bugging her or retribution. It was so much worse. "You don't trust me."

"Based on your behavior, give me one good reason why I should."

"That was personal," she said. "This is business."

"Most people don't check their character at the door when they come to work."

She leaned forward and rested her arms on her desk. "You really think I'd walk out and leave you in the lurch?"

"Why wouldn't I?"

Okay, that *had* been a bad way to phrase it. "I'm good at my job," she defended.

"You wouldn't be here otherwise. But you can't do it if you're not here."

She was stunned that he believed her capable of walking out on her work. "If you think that, why didn't you simply terminate my contract?"

"Believe me, if I could have you'd be gone. But that would cause media attention, too."

She struggled for composure as emotions zinged through her. She'd sort them out later. "Isn't publicity what you're after?"

"Not that kind. You're a high-profile employee and we have a past. Making a change like that would spook the investors. I can't afford to make any move that could be construed as a chink in my armor. The money guys want to see strong, steady leadership and that's what they'll get."

Anger smoldered in his eyes and told her he wasn't over their past, in spite of what he'd said. But his showing up every day wasn't about seeing her. He was keeping an eye on her.

Geneva really didn't want to be any more involved with him than she already was. Especially with another wedding-related event. She'd made her choices; she had her regrets. She didn't need more of his presence than she already had. But this was another choice out of her hands.

"All right, Michael. I'll be sure to keep you informed about everything from tablecloth thread count to font size on the invitations."

"Then we're clear."

"Crystal."

Silly her for the tiniest little hope that his dropping by every day was a good thing. She hadn't even realized the hope was there until he'd crushed it under his cold, calculated mistrust. However much she didn't want to be fair, she had to admit he had his reasons. He might not mean this as retribution, but the result was effective. She was good at what she did. Her job was the only part of her life she trusted. And he'd just taken that away.

Michael pressed the call button on the elevator, then turned to survey the lobby while he waited. The marble floors were tough enough to withstand foot traffic, yet elegant. Several crystal chandeliers winked down on the leather love seats and chairs. Graceful cherry wood tables topped with fresh flowers were cleverly arranged around the large area. It was a place he would be proud to put his parents' names on at the Towers dedication.

Then, breezing through the revolving lobby door, he saw Geneva. The woman who'd refused the Sullivan name.

She smiled at someone and Michael felt a pull in his gut—the same tight, tensing of muscles he'd felt the very first time he'd seen her and knew he had to have her. Her smile could drop a man's IQ into the idiot range and he'd been no exception. Her sleeveless white dress caressed every luscious curve of the body he'd once caressed, the body that had held and lost his child. He still carried that pain; he always would.

He was used to success; Geneva had been his first failure. He hadn't asked for the attraction that had turned him inside out, but a lot of things happened in his life that he hadn't asked for. He'd slipped up by letting her become important. He hadn't gotten where he was by making the same mistake twice.

If only she wasn't so damn beautiful. If only she hadn't walked out. If only he didn't still want her with the same intensity as the first time he'd seen her. But he was working on that. The success of the Towers had forced him into keeping her around, but he intended to use the situation to his advantage. They would spend time together and when the dust settled, he would feel nothing for her.

The elevator doors opened, then closed again when he didn't step inside. He watched Geneva stop and study the three-dimensional display of his residential tower project.

He crossed the lobby and stood beside her. "I've been looking for you."

"Here I am," she said, glancing up at him. "Are you checking up on me?"

"Do I need to?"

"Only you can answer that." Her eyes narrowed. "I'm sorry. I forgot to inform you that it was a working lunch."

"Oh?"

"Yes. I was looking at chapels."

"And?"

"I made an executive decision and ruled out the drive-through Elvis chapel, the Liberace Museum, a houseboat on Lake Mead, or the hot air balloon over the Strip."

Her sarcasm let him know what she thought of his micromanaging. He had a momentary flicker of admiration for her sassiness, then shut it down. "Good decision. The balloon would certainly pose some logistical challenges."

"No kidding. My fear of heights for one."

When her full lips curved into a tight smile that

unleashed her dimples, he felt the blood drain from his brain and head for points south. Then her words sank in.

"I didn't know you were afraid of heights."

"Yeah." She shuddered. "Anyway, I still have a list of places to check out. When I narrow it down, I'll let Teri know. And you, of course."

"Good."

She stared at him for several moments, before her gaze skittered away. "Well, lunch is over," she said, then started across the lobby.

He fell into step beside her as she walked to the elevators and pushed the up button.

She glanced at him. "You said you were looking for me."

He nodded and slid his hands into the pockets of his slacks. "Teri told me about you repaying the wedding costs."

She looked surprised. "You didn't know?"

"Dex just told her. He's the money guy and he holds a grudge."

"Is he the only one?"

"If you're asking whether or not I have feelings of resentment, the answer is no."

A flat-out lie. He knew because of the satisfaction and enjoyment he felt at keeping her guessing. And other feelings? Definitely he had feelings—resentment, revenge, regret—topping the list.

Geneva watched him carefully, as if she were

searching for a sign of his sincerity. "Good," she said, nodding. "No hard feelings."

The elevator dinged, and the doors whispered open. Geneva stepped inside and Michael joined her. What was it about being alone with this woman in an elevator that made him want to pull her into his arms? And why still this woman? At the moment, lust trumped revenge.

He could smell her perfume and remembered the scent that always made him want to taste the hollow just below her ear. It was a dangerous thought and not exactly the way this plan of his was supposed to work.

"Why did you pay me back for the wedding? It didn't happen."

"That's why."

"Meaning?" he asked, irritated.

She sighed. "It was my fault, Michael. I had doubts and they didn't just surface the day of the ceremony. I should have called everything off before—" She stopped and caught her top lip between her teeth. "Before I did. Before we lost more than just the deposits."

"I don't need the money."

"But I needed to pay it back."

"So it's about you?"

"If that's the way you want to look at it. Yes, I didn't go through with the ceremony. Yes, there were a lot of people who saw me not go through with it. Yes, the reporters pestered us mercilessly to find out why. Definitely I'm sorry I put you through all of the above. But no way would I let you foot the bill for my mistake and somehow use it against me."

He was stunned that she'd believe such a thing. "Did I ever give you reason to think I would do that?"

"We weren't together all that long, Michael. I don't know if *you* would. However, I do know some people would."

"What are you talking about?"

"It doesn't matter." When her purse strap slid down her arm, she settled it more firmly on her shoulder. "The point is, I chose to stop the wedding. And there was fallout from the decision."

"Decisions have a way of biting you in the ass."

"Yeah. Decisions." She met his gaze and hers was filled with the hurt she struggled to hide with anger. "And I'll tell you how you'll know I won't walk out on my responsibilities to you. I mortgaged my condo to pay you back. I need the job. And I don't turn my back on the hard stuff."

"Neither do I."

"I'm not accusing you of anything."

"Not in so many words, but the implication is there."

"I didn't mean to imply anything. No one knows better than me that you do the right thing." The elevator stopped on the floor housing the executive suites and she stepped out. "But sometimes, Michael, the right thing can be a mistake."

He watched her walk away, puzzled by what

she'd said. How could doing the right thing ever be a mistake?

Wasn't he working with her for the good of the project? So far that decision was biting him in the ass. Doing the right thing was pushing his desire into the danger zone.

CHAPTER THREE

GENEVA grabbed her purse from the bottom drawer of her desk, then stepped into the outer office where her assistant was typing up notes.

"Chloe?"

"Yes, boss?" Chloe Milton was a blue-eyed redhead with a freckle-splashed nose and sass to spare.

"I'm going to be out of the office this afternoon."

"I got your note. Too bad you're not playing hooky. Or, better yet, playing with fire."

That only happened when Michael was around, Geneva thought. And he wouldn't be. She planned to sneak out before he could drop in and demand to know if the chapels had pews, chairs or picnic tables.

She hadn't seen him for a week, not since she'd told him doing the right thing can be a mistake. An army of psychiatrists would have a field day figuring out that remark. Michael Sullivan? He probably thought she was one Jimmy short of a pair of Choos and had steered clear of her, considering himself lucky that five minutes of humiliation had saved him a whole lifetime of weird. But the change in his daily visits made her uneasy.

"I put in a call to Melina St. George in New York," she briefed her assistant. "I want to talk to her about doing the food for the grand opening of Sullivan Towers."

"Isn't she the chef who did that celebrity event in Santa Barbara?"

"That's the one," Geneva confirmed. "If she calls, let me know and I'll get right back to her."

"Will do, boss."

"See you tomorrow. I won't be back before you leave for the day."

Blue eyes widened in surprise. "So your note only says you're checking out chapels. I'm assuming you're not looking for a religious experience?"

"Hardly." Not since Michael. She sighed. It seemed all thoughts led back to him. Geneva wasn't sure how to stop that. It had been so much easier when she didn't have to see him at all.

"Who's getting married?" Chloe asked. "Anyone I know?"

"Teri Sullivan."

"She asked you to plan it?" Chloe couldn't have looked more shocked if Geneva had stripped naked and jumped into Bellagio's dancing water.

"Michael did the actual asking."

"That's diabolical."

"Revenge has nothing to do with it," Geneva countered.

"Who said anything about revenge?" Chloe stared skeptically. "But now that you mention it—what fantasyland are you living in? What other reason could he have?"

"I'm good at my job?" Geneva said wryly.

"That's true. But revenge has got to be right up there at the top of his list."

"We both know Michael could have let me go. Instead he put me in charge of two projects." Geneva could do paranoia on her own and really didn't need it reinforced.

"Payback can take many forms." Chloe nodded sagely.

That had already occurred to Geneva, but she did owe Michael. She'd promised to do whatever she could to help him succeed and wouldn't go back on her word. She'd show him that she wouldn't let him down again.

"Bye, Chlo."

Geneva stopped at the elevator and pushed the down button. She heard someone behind her and turned.

"Where are you off to?" Michael asked. "A working lunch?"

Damn. She'd almost made it. Did he have a homing device on her? "Actually I'm checking out more chapels."

"Good. I'm glad I ran into you. I'll come along."

Was it technically running into her if he did it deliberately? Clearly he had an agenda, she just wasn't sure what he had in mind. "Along?"

"I'd like some input. We can take the limo."

Geneva hoped he wasn't serious or it was going to be a very long afternoon. "Thanks anyway, Michael. But I need my car. I have things to do. Appointments," she said vaguely.

"I'll take you where you need to go."

"I understand you want details. But I'm the wedding planner. I'm supposed to be doing the legwork."

"The thing is, I like legwork," he said, his gaze dropping to her hem.

Geneva resisted the urge to look down. She already knew her skirt was short, but now she wished it was a suit of armor.

"Michael, this is my job," she insisted, looking up at him. "However much you feel the need to micromanage, you must have more important things to do than weed out wedding chapels."

"Nothing is more important than my sister." His eyes darkened.

"You don't need to supervise. I have nothing to report yet. I know you have no reason to trust me, but I'll do my best to make sure Teri has exactly what she wants," Geneva assured him.

"There are some things she wants that you can't do. Like the family touch."

And she wasn't family. She'd almost been a Sullivan. But almost only counted in horseshoes and hand grenades.

"This is important to me," he said. "Teri doesn't have her mother to help shop for her wedding dress. She doesn't have her father to walk her down the aisle."

"Teri has you." Geneva hadn't meant to say that, but the words popped out. Probably because Geneva felt a twinge of remorse for being so cynical. Michael was many things, but a jerk wasn't one of them.

He'd been both mother and father to his sister and he'd done a fine job raising her when he was practically a boy himself. He was a good man. It would be so much easier if he wasn't, if she could simply dislike him. But she couldn't. And that was the biggest problem of all.

He looked down. "And I don't want her to forget that I'll always be there for her, especially on her wedding day."

Geneva nodded. "I'll keep that in mind."

That wasn't a lie. Michael was always on her mind, whether she wanted him there or not. But she saw the shadows in his eyes for a split second and the expression tugged at her heart. This wasn't about her.

The elevator dinged just before the doors opened. Michael looked at her. "Geneva, stop arguing and get in."

She got in and a few minutes later was sitting beside him in the back of his limousine. The luxurious interior was leather, plush carpet and the spicy scent of Michael. As they pulled out from beneath the covered hotel entrance, tinted windows shielded them from the desert heat and curious stares, because limos in Vegas signaled a possible celebrity sighting.

Geneva glanced at Michael and knew there wasn't anything to shield her from him. His showing up unexpectedly was probably part of his ongoing strategy to mess with her mind. How annoying that it was working.

She stole another glance and noticed he was casually dressed in a black knit shirt and khaki slacks. Another good look, although she doubted he had a bad one.

Then she thought about what he'd said. The words about family hung heavy in the air and she searched for something to break the tension.

"You know," she started, "I don't think you ever met my family."

He frowned, thinking. "Now that you mention it… Why is that?"

"It's a long story. Suffice it to say that if my parents had been at our wedding, my bombshell would have been just a footnote to their hostilities."

"Oh?"

"Mom would have argued with Dad that her husband should walk me down the aisle and give me away."

"Even though he's your stepfather?"

"She'd have come up with a reason and dug her heels in. And Dad—" She shook her head. "If she said white, he'd say black."

"Fight do they?"

"Like the Montagues and Capulets," she agreed. In her own story the only casualty had been her heart, by her own hand. But it was still a tragic ending thanks to the baggage she carried, a by-product of her childhood. "I always thought it was ironic that they named me after a city in a country that prides itself on remaining neutral. The two of them can't be in the same room and have a civil conversation. But it was worse when they were actually married."

"How long ago did they divorce?"

"A long time. I was about ten," she said, remembering the fear and uncertainty she'd felt, huddled in her room with her hands over her ears, trying to shut out the fighting, the nasty accusations and name-calling. She met his gaze, trying hard to hide the remembered pain. "But it was for the best. Things were ugly between the two of them for a very long time. And they kept trying to make it work because of me."

"Is that what you meant when you said sometimes the right thing can be a mistake?"

Actually she'd meant Michael's reason for going through with their wedding. But it would be best to let him think that she'd been talking about her parents.

"Yeah," she agreed. "That's what I meant."

He studied her. "You never told me about growing up in a battle zone."

"No?"

She frowned as she thought back. It was hard to believe she'd never mentioned her traumatic childhood. Then she remembered the combustible attraction she and Michael had shared. When they'd been in the same room, sparks flew. Everything about their affair had been red-hot and they'd been consumed only with each other. They'd done everything with their mouths *except* talk.

It was inevitable that the passion would burn out, that the embers would turn to ashes. If there'd been more than the baby holding them together, Michael wouldn't have disappeared without a word. If the wedding had gone forward, they'd have ended up hating each other. Divorce wars would have been inevitable. That fate was part of what had scared her about marrying him.

She didn't want to end up hating Michael. She also didn't want to be attracted to him, but so far she hadn't figured out how to make her attraction stop.

She hoped he would think she meant her childhood when she said, "I guess I'm just trying to put the past behind me."

At Geneva's direction the limo driver guided the big car into the parking lot of a white building on the corner of Las Vegas and Sahara Boulevards. She and

Michael had spent hours touring chapels and now she couldn't resist a little payback of her own. He'd wanted to tag along? She'd show him some legwork.

The sun had gone down but the darkness didn't quite hide the potholes in the parking lot and the dinginess of the buildings on this side of the street. Just across the boulevard, neon lights glittered on the dome over the Sahara Hotel entrance and the camel that was part of the property milieu.

Geneva's door opened and Michael held it while she slipped out—trying not to flash too much thigh as her skirt slid up. She was certain he didn't miss a thing when it did.

He glanced around and lifted one eyebrow when he noticed the sign on the building. "The Garden of Love."

She struggled to maintain an innocent expression. "What do you think?"

"It gives a whole new meaning to the phrase 'weeding out chapels.'"

She refused to laugh. There was no laughter in payback. "I still want to check it out."

"Why?" He looked skeptical.

"It won't take long."

They walked into a small lobby filled with people. To the right was a wall with a sliding window and she tapped on the glass. A teenage boy opened it. His dark hair was shiny with product and worked into what looked like porcupine needles all over his head. Geneva would bet if he stood, his baggy jeans would reveal his brand of boxers, which was way more than she wanted to know.

He pulled off the earphones plugged into his MP3 player. "Welcome to The Garden of Love."

"Thanks," she said. "I'd like to look at your facility. I'm planning a wedding." That was the truth.

"For you and the dude?" The kid stared at Michael and seemed unimpressed by the man's glare.

"No." She was definitely unimpressed by Michael's glare. Maybe next time he would leave her alone and let her do her job.

"That's cool." The kid gave her a once-over, interest evident in his eyes. "Take a look."

She glanced around the busy lobby. "Are you sure we won't be in the way?"

"Nah. It's always like this. We got weddings scheduled every half hour all night. No one'll notice. Just so you know, the deluxe wedding is around a hundred and fifty dollars. That includes rings and a limo." He put the earphones back in and adjusted the volume.

Michael frowned at a line of people dressed in everything from red sequins to ripped-at-the-knees jeans as they filed from one room into another.

He looked down at her. "Is there a point to this?"

Definitely, she thought. "Come on, Michael."

She took his arm and tugged him to the end of the line moving steadily through a maze to the ceremony room. Once inside, they took seats in the back on a low, very hard bench.

Michael leaned over and said in a husky whisper, "With a wedding every half hour, I guess they're not overly concerned about spectator comfort."

"Don't be so grumpy." Glancing down, she said, "Genuine plastic brick floor."

He leaned close. "To go with the genuine plastic rock formation covering the lectern."

His breath tickled her ear and raised tingles over her skin. "Look. I think the fan blowing on the clear plastic sheets in front of the blue background to simulate a waterfall is a particularly nice touch."

"Not as nice as the real wood lattice covering the walls."

"Set off to perfection by the plastic roses tucked into it," she agreed.

"And to think you get all this for a hundred and fifty bucks."

The look of mock sincerity on his face was so cute, so funny, so completely unexpected, so utterly charming. Geneva slapped a hand over her mouth to stifle the laughter. Just then a bride walked down the aisle in a red, crushed velvet dress. When the coast was clear, Geneva slipped out of the room, with Michael right behind her. In the now empty lobby, the two of them started laughing.

This was the first time they'd laughed together in over a year. The thought stopped her cold, but the feelings simmering through her were all about heat.

It was too intimate, she thought, struggling to

catch her breath, and not because of the laughter. "This place is priceless. Tacky times ten."

He nodded as he looked around. "Dex would like the price. He knows a deal when he sees one."

"Look," she said, nodding toward a doorway. "People are crowded into that room. Let's see what's going on."

"Okay." Michael took her hand and led her across the matted down, powder-blue carpet.

Geneva was startled that he'd gotten into the spirit of things, but even more surprised at how good her hand felt tucked into his. And she was amazed by the fact that such a harmless touch could make her heart stutter. On second thought, the touch wasn't so harmless.

She slid her hand from his as they peeked into the room and saw the next bride in a knee-length white slip dress. The groom stood by her side and they couldn't stop smiling at each other.

Michael looked down at her, his expression wry. "What's next? The drive-through chapel with the Elvis impersonator?"

"You have no romance in your soul," she scoffed.

"I have as much as the next guy," he defended. "But whoever decorated this place is obviously romance-challenged."

"Who cares about decorations? Look at them," she said, indicating the couple waiting to pledge their lives to each other.

"What?"

"They only have eyes for each other." She sighed and backed out of the doorway. "They wouldn't care if they got married in a chapel or a coat closet. Love is all that matters." What the heck did she know about love? And she'd actually said that to Michael, of all people. Abruptly she turned away. "We should go."

"Yeah."

He rested his hand at the small of her back to guide her out. It was a courteous gesture, so very much like the Michael she remembered. She could feel the heat of his fingers burn through the silky material of her blouse. He held the door as she walked outside into the warm summer evening. She pulled air into her lungs, trying to steady her breathing, not an easy thing to do with Michael still touching her.

They walked down the ramp to the parking lot at the bottom. Before she could keep going to the waiting limo, Michael put a hand on her arm. "I have one question."

"What?" She forced herself to meet his gaze.

"Why did you bring me here?"

Why indeed. Finally she said, "To mess with your mind."

A gleam stole into his eyes. "Is that wise, Geneva? You won't win."

It was just the two of them, the moon, the stars and the warm breeze. Something in his expression announced danger ahead, but she couldn't move. It was a look she remembered from the first time she'd seen him and suddenly Michael was a whisper away, their bodies barely brushing. He tunneled his fingers into her hair and held her face as he lowered his mouth to hers.

The voice in her head was shouting run and don't look back. But her heart was already anticipating the heat as his lips generated sparks that burst into familiar flames. She couldn't stop herself any more than she could stop breathing. All she knew was an overpowering need to kiss him back.

She opened her mouth and thought she heard him groan, although the blood pounding in her ears made it hard to tell. He pushed the advantage and plunged inside, stroking with his tongue, wrapping her in the taste, touch and scent of him. Jolts of excitement sparked through her, zapping her system with a thousand volts of awareness. She really didn't want to, but she was feeling again.

It was as if her body had gone into hibernation and had just been waiting for Michael Sullivan's risky brand of magic to awaken her. All she could think was that she wanted the kiss to go on forever. She'd barely thought the thought when he dragged his mouth from hers and let out a long breath.

"Well," she said shakily.

"Deep subject." His voice was husky, low and laced with lingering desire.

She pressed her lips together, still tasting his kiss.

"So was that part of the Sullivan-get-even-and-stay-on-top strategy? Or the forgive-and-forget plan?"

"Why don't we call it kiss and make up?"

"How about none of the above?"

With his knuckle, Michael nudged her chin up until she met his gaze. "How about that."

Her heart was beating too fast and the look in his eyes told her he knew it. That was bad. If she'd seen it coming, maybe she could have prepared, but she hadn't. And that's when it hit her.

What if he wasn't micromanaging at all? What if he planned to make her fall for him again, then walk away? Don't get mad, get even. What if that kiss was the next step in his plan? And what if it was working?

She'd been barely able to resist the Michael Sullivan brand of charm. But that was before his kiss awakened desires she'd spent the last year trying to forget.

CHAPTER FOUR

MICHAEL wondered what the hell he'd been thinking when he'd kissed Geneva.

The answer was, he hadn't been thinking—at least not with his head. From that first day in his office, he'd wanted to taste her again, just to get it out of his system. Then she'd taken him on that wild-goose chase to the Garden of Love. The kiss had started out as a way to show her who was boss, but it had turned into something else completely. It was a damn, stupid thing to do.

It had been a week since that lapse of self-control. When he wasn't thinking about kissing her again, Michael was still kicking himself from one side of the Vegas Valley to the other. Focusing on Sullivan Towers managed to push everything else from his mind for long periods of time. In fact, work had always been his salvation. It wasn't coincidence that when fate dumped on his personal life, his business affairs couldn't be better.

But Geneva had an annoying habit of sneaking into his mind. In the middle of a meeting. While he was trying to assimilate the information on a spreadsheet. In dreams where he held her in his arms again. Just because he hadn't seen her since The Garden of Love didn't mean he could avoid her in his thoughts.

Michael walked into his office and picked up the messages on his desk. One was from Geneva. Just seeing her name sent sparks of heat flashing through him, which was irritating. And frustrating. After a marathon lunch meeting dealing with the rising costs of building materials and fuel, his eyes felt like they were glazing over. A workout was what he needed to clear his mind.

He grabbed the duffel bag with shorts, T-shirt and athletic shoes that he kept in the closet and headed to the company fitness center. In the men's locker room he changed out of his suit and tie, then stretched before going to the equipment area that held treadmills, stationary bikes, weight machines and free weights. Smoked glass and low-E windows filtered out the heat that was a part of Vegas in the summer. On the street below, fans dispersed moisture from misters onto the pedestrians walking up and down the Strip.

The underlying hum drew his attention to the woman just shutting down a treadmill. At lunch time, this room was crowded, but it was way after that now and he'd expected to be alone. When she turned, Michael recognized Geneva and lust sucker punched him.

She did a double-take before wariness settled in her expression. "Michael."

"Hi." He moved closer and rested an elbow on the treadmill handgrip.

He was accustomed to seeing her in professional suits, pants and blazers, and even the short skirt he'd last seen her wearing that revealed her spectacular legs. But the midriff baring top and skintight spandex shorts she had on now left very little of her amazing body to the imagination. Although he didn't need to imagine. He'd seen every square inch of her bare flesh.

"I was just leaving," she said.

"Not on my account, I hope. How are you?" he asked.

"Fine." She bent and grabbed the towel beside her, then dried her face. "You?"

"Great."

Wanting Geneva was a given when he looked at her. But Michael waited for the jab of resentment that always followed the punch of desire. The fact that he had to wait for it at all wasn't good. Kissing Geneva hadn't been his biggest mistake after all, it had been going with her in the first place. Because she'd told him personal things that would leave scars on a little girl.

No wonder she'd thought twice about marriage. And, damn it, he didn't want to cut her any slack about why she'd done what she had. He wanted to resent her. He counted on that to keep him from doing something else stupid.

She draped the towel around her neck. "You know the news of Teri's engagement was released?"

"Yeah."

"And the media has the information that I'm the wedding planner?"

"Yup."

"Good." She nodded. "Actually I'm glad we ran into each other." She didn't look glad; she looked tense. "I tried to get you earlier."

He remembered the message. "What's up?"

"I wanted to run something by you. But I can call your office later."

"I've got time now."

As she talked, she was stretching from side to side, keeping loose the muscles she'd already warmed up. The way her body looked and the twisting action warmed him up without moving a muscle.

He struggled to concentrate on what she was saying. If there was a God in heaven, the words would actually get to his brain. "You have my undivided attention."

"I've been approached for an interview by a prime time entertainment program."

"You agreed, right?"

"Conditionally," she hedged.

"What condition?"

"That you're okay with it." She studied him for a reaction.

"We knew this would happen. We're counting on it," he reminded her.

"I know. But if I go through with it, there's no going back."

He didn't want to go back. Because the hell of it was that just looking at her took him back to a time when he'd thought he had the world in his hands. Then she'd reminded him he shouldn't count on the good stuff.

She leaned back, stretching out her abdominal muscles. Now that he'd dialed down the lust factor and was no longer in danger of swallowing his tongue, he saw clearly that there wasn't an ounce of fat on her body. That's not to say she wasn't in great shape when they'd been together. But he'd been intimately familiar with every slender line, every mouthwatering curve and she looked different now—toned and sculpted in a way she hadn't been a year ago.

"Do the interview."

"Okay." She took another sip of water. "Just so you know, I plan to take full responsibility for the nonwedding and the official word will be that we're still good friends."

"Don't forget to mention Sullivan Towers."

She grinned. "If they don't ask—and that's a big if—I'll steer the conversation to you and the project."

"Good."

"The other thing is the engagement party."

"What about it?"

"I just got the guest list from Teri. I'll e-mail it to you when I'm back at my desk. I need you to look it over right away for additions or corrections. The invitations have to go out in the next day or two."

"Okay," he agreed.

She seemed completely focused on work. And why should that annoy him? Probably because he couldn't seem to take his eyes off her mouth and wondered if the earth had moved only for him, or if she'd felt something, too.

"By the way," he said, "You're going to look terrific on TV."

She scoffed. "They say the camera adds ten pounds. You might want to reserve judgment—right after you get your eyes checked."

"There's nothing wrong with my judgment or my vision. You look great. Different."

"I'm still the same."

Since he was beginning to realize how little he'd known about her "the same" didn't mean a lot. He folded his arms over his chest as he studied her. "Yes and no. You're really ripped. Toned. Sexy as hell."

The pink in her cheeks wasn't entirely from her workout. "I've done some sessions with a personal trainer. Luke."

"It shows," he said evenly. The question was

followed by an irrational stab of jealousy. Who the hell was Luke?

"He's taught me a lot about fitness. It's a delicate balancing act between proper nutrition, regular exercise, rest and relaxation."

"So you've given up your two best friends?"

"Who?" she asked, puzzled.

"Ben & Jerry."

"Ah. Ice cream." She laughed, flashing her world-class dimples. "I haven't given it up entirely, sad to say. But I don't consider it one of the major food groups anymore. And if I indulge, it's no frills. Plain vanilla. No crushed up candy bar."

"I'm impressed."

She shrugged. "No big deal. I simply wanted to improve my health. When I was pregnant—"

"What?" he prompted, gentling his tone because of the sudden sadness on her face.

"It's just—" Shadows turned her eyes a deep, beautiful green. "I could have been in better shape. That's all."

If Michael hadn't seen her smile moments ago, he might have missed the sorrow in her eyes, but it stood out in stark contrast. He realized she blamed herself for losing the baby.

"It wasn't your fault, Geneva," he said, trying to give comfort even as his own remembered pain sliced deep. The idea of having a child, being a father... He'd been nervous, excited and over-the-moon happy. A baby with Geneva. Life didn't get any better. And he'd been right. It got worse because he'd lost them both.

But the grief lingering in her eyes disturbed him. "The doctor said it wasn't anything you did or didn't do. No one knows why those things happen."

"But it happened to me," she said. "Who else is there to blame?"

Had she carried this self-reproach around for the last year? Pain he could understand. But assuming responsibility for something that was out of her control made him want to take her in his arms and hold her.

The need to console her felt far more dangerous than kissing her and that was why he didn't try to stop her when she walked away.

Geneva hadn't known Michael was so observant. Or that she'd fixate on his words. He'd noticed the changes in her body and said she was sexy as hell. None of that was why she'd made a decision to be healthier. She would give up the rosy glow of his compliment in a heartbeat if she could hold her baby in her arms.

She leaned back in her desk chair and rubbed her tired eyes. The thing was, she'd lost *their* baby—hers and Michael's. He'd done the right thing that night in the E.R. He'd held her while she cried. The next day he'd thrown himself into work and the wedding.

That her thoughts were slipping back into the past

told her it was way past time to go home. She straightened and pulled her chair closer to the computer, then clicked the mouse to save the file she'd been working on. If only she could click on these thoughts and put them away as easily. Better yet, hit the delete key.

Michael had tried to comfort her in the gym—seven days ago and counting. She hadn't seen him since. Absence makes the heart grow fonder.

"Damn it," she said, disgusted with herself.

She wished she'd never brought up the pregnancy. It was the link to their past, the only reason he'd asked her to marry him. She'd thought about it ever since their last conversation and wished she could take back the words. They had skewed her concentration. As much as she'd like to bail out, it wasn't the contract that stopped her now. She had something to prove. Michael didn't trust her, but she wouldn't let him down again.

"Hi," he said. Speaking of the devil… He was lounging in her office doorway, all rumpled-at-the-end-of-the-day, sexy CEO. "What are you still doing here?"

"I work here?" It was part question, part statement. "Unless you changed your mind and decided to fire me." She could joke about that now because she knew it wasn't part of his plan.

"Fire my star?"

"Star? The light of your world?"

"My heavenly body?" One dark eyebrow lifted as his smile teased. Surely he wasn't flirting.

This was risky territory, but she couldn't help smiling back. "Was there a reason you stopped by? Or are you just here to torture me?"

"My reason is job related. Teasing you is just one of the perks."

He lifted one broad shoulder in a careless shrug. He'd abandoned his suit coat, loosened his tie and rolled the long sleeves of his white dress shirt to just below his elbows. It was a good look, masculine, and gave a girl a pretty good view of those strong forearms.

"So what's the deal?" she asked, when she was sure of a normal tone.

"I saw the interview on *Celebrity Access*."

Geneva winced. She'd refused to look at it. Media interviews weren't a new thing, but she couldn't stand watching herself, listening to her own voice, critiquing her words and wishing she'd said something more—or less. But he'd called her his "star."

"Dare I ask what you thought?"

"You were good." He didn't sound surprised, merely pleased with the results.

"It was okay?"

"If you're fishing for compliments, I can oblige. It was better than okay. I don't know how you managed, but I lost count of how many times you mentioned Sullivan Towers."

"So they aired all of it," she said.

"I'm not sure. There was a teaser about more of Geneva Porter's revealing interview on the next *Celebrity Access*."

"Good. They'll repeat a lot of what I said, then focus on a different slant. That's excellent. You never know what will get taken out of context or cut completely."

He moved closer to her desk and rested a hip on one corner. "Speaking of context, I found especially intriguing your responses to questions about you and me."

"What specifically?" She tried to remember. There were so many.

"The ones about us working together. The possibility of being a couple again."

"Oh. Those questions." Geneva had expected to be interrogated about their past and current relationship. But the possibility of them being a couple again hadn't occurred to her—except for one, brief, breathless moment while Michael was kissing her.

When she met his gaze and saw the gleam in his eyes, she knew he was remembering the kiss, too.

"Yeah. Those questions," he said. "Your answers were just vague enough to create more questions."

Always best to tell the truth, and that's what she'd done. But it was also true that no one had more questions about her and Michael than she did. "Good. Then I was a loyal team player and let the press come up with yet another angle to the story. More publicity for Sullivans."

"And if the press cries 'publicity stunt?'"

She shrugged and picked up a pen on her desk, toying with it to keep her nervous fingers busy. He knew as well as she did that it was, in fact, all about publicity. So what was he asking her? If there was something between them? If they needed to beef up that slant and make their relationship a pretense?

"Their speculation isn't our problem. And there's not a whole lot we can do about it. The press is using us as much as we're using them." She met his gaze.

"So when life gives you lemons..."

His gaze darkened and being the focus of all that intensity made her nervous. He didn't trust her, but she didn't trust him right back. It was time for a little humor to bail her out. "Ah, how the mighty have fallen."

"Oh?"

She sighed dramatically. "From star to lemon in a nanosecond."

When he laughed, the sound of it burrowed inside her and melted places she was trying very hard to keep frozen. His face took on a whole new charm, fascination and temptation. A frowning Michael Sullivan was drop-dead gorgeous. Smiling he was practically irresistible. Geneva felt the power of it chipping away at her resolve. Keep it about business, she thought.

"I'm glad you were pleased with the interview. Was there something else?"

"Are you trying to get rid of me?" The tone was teasing, but the edge was back.

"I wouldn't dream of it. You're my boss."

He met her gaze. "And in that capacity I say again, why are you here so late?"

"I have work to finish up before I go home."

He looked at the pile of papers on her desk. "No date tonight?"

"No." Why would he ask that?

"That's hard to believe."

"I don't know why it should be."

"Then I'll tell you. You're beautiful, smart, funny—and single."

Her pulse jumped and just like that breathing was a challenge. This was getting way too complicated. She tried to be all business and he backed her into a personal corner. Which fueled her suspicions about his motives. All she knew to do was come out swinging.

She rested an elbow on the desk and settled her chin in her palm as she met his gaze. "I could ask you the same thing, Michael. You're too good-looking for your own good, smarter than the average bachelor, and you've got a passable sense of humor when you choose to use it. How come you're not doing the singles scene at the Ghost Bar? Or Light? Or The House of Blues? If Las Vegas has anything, it's an abundance of clubs for single guys trolling."

"Trolling?" One corner of his mouth lifted. "I don't think I've ever had the pleasure."

"You should try it."

"I'm not interested. What's your excuse?"

Keep it light, she reminded herself. Tricky, because her excuse was the same. She hadn't been interested. Not in dating, trolling or anything else with the opposite sex. Not since Michael.

"My boss keeps me too busy for a social life."

"Your boss sounds like a workaholic. Let's take him out back and beat the crap out of him." He flashed his very white teeth in a fleeting grin.

"As appealing as that sounds, he's still my boss. And messing up his pretty face would be such a shame. Not to mention the whole hostile work environment thing."

"Hmm." His dark eyebrows pulled together. "That would be bad."

More than bad, hot. And getting hotter by the second.

"I swear you're up-to-date on all details. So, unless there's something else about work to discuss, you need to leave me alone. I've got stuff to do."

Michael stood and slid his hands into the pockets of his slacks. "Have you thought about finding another boss?"

She studied his expression, wondering if there was a deeper meaning to their banter in general and that question in particular. Finding no clue to his thoughts, she said, "Even though he's demanding, exacting and works too hard, I sincerely like my boss." Nothing succeeds like the truth.

"I think it's safe to say that sentiment is reciprocated," he said carefully.

There'd been a lot of reciprocating during that kiss, she thought. And she didn't trust it. If she could just get him to go away, everything would be fine.

She met his gaze and waved her hand in a shooing motion. "Okay. Now hit the road before I get really behind in my work and my boss decides to let me go after all."

Michael stopped in her doorway and glanced over his shoulder. "If he fired you, he'd be an idiot."

Then he was gone and Geneva let out a long breath.

Spontaneous combustion was a very real danger every time she and Michael were in the same room mostly because there was abundant fuel in the dry brush of her emotions. He was the spark that could make her go up in flames. She'd known it about thirty seconds after walking into his office that day. She'd also survived a lonely, post-Michael scorched heart.

She wouldn't let him put her through that a second time.

CHAPTER FIVE

GENEVA wondered where the last six weeks had gone. Probably into the incredible number of hours she'd spent planning this engagement party. So much for a little food, a little drink and a few invitations. But it had all come together. She'd already done interviews for *People* magazine and *In Style*. Before the guests arrived, she was giving a reporter and photographer from *Celebrity Access* a tour of the banquet room on the top floor of the Sullivan Hotel.

Shannon Robinson looked around and sighed. "This room looks magical. The red roses on the tables are fabulous. It looks like fairyland."

"Thank you. It's my job to find the most talented people."

Geneva loved the way the arrangements had been done, low and round, so that the guests wouldn't have to look around and through them to have a conversation. The roses marched up the center of each long table—cutting a red swath through the sea of white linen. At each place setting, the appropriate silverware bracketed a large silver plate where servers would set the china. Flowers and greenery were everywhere in the room and small, white lights had been artfully draped for a magical, romantic effect.

The photographer posed Geneva in front of the bank of floor to ceiling windows looking out over the glittering neon lights of Las Vegas. As many times as she could mention it without sounding obnoxious, she told the reporter that the bride's brother was building Sullivan Towers on the property adjacent to the hotel.

"Geneva, you look fabulous. Doesn't she, Danny?"

The photographer nodded as he looked through his lens. "The camera loves her."

"I'm glad you think so."

"Your dress is stunning. Who are you wearing?"

Geneva had always thought the question sounded weird, but knew couture designers needed publicity, too.

"Vera Wang." The floor-length black taffeta crisscrossed over her abdomen and the V-neck bodice created cleavage. But her favorite thing was the poofy skirt that swished as she walked.

"It's stunning," Shannon said. "You look amazing."

"I couldn't have said it better myself." Michael's voice emerged from just beyond the photographer's light.

"Michael, you're just in time." Before she caught herself, Geneva glowed from his compliment. "This is

Shannon Robinson and her photographer, Danny, from *Celebrity Access*. As the brother of the bride and best friend of the groom, you should be in the pictures."

"Nice to meet you," he said, shaking hands. Then he was beside her and the expression in his eyes took her breath away. As the camera flashed, he whispered in her ear, "You clean up pretty good, Ms. Porter."

"You're not so bad yourself," she answered, giving him a thorough once-over. In the black suit he was male perfection and, since the sight of him rendered her speechless, he'd have to pick up the slack for the rest of this interview.

"Armani?" Shannon asked him.

"Good eye." Michael grinned his charming grin.

Shannon blinked several times, then recovered her voice as she looked from Geneva to Michael. "Any chance the two of you are hooking up again?"

"We're working together on several projects," Michael said smoothly.

"I meant as a couple. Geneva? Any comment?"

"Yes," she said, glancing up at Michael. There was a question in his eyes. "Right now all of our energy is focused on Teri Sullivan's wedding and the grand opening of the Sullivan Towers sales office in about eight weeks."

"What about after that?"

"We'll still be good friends." Michael took her hand and slipped it into the bend of his elbow, signaling an end to the interview.

The gesture would keep them guessing, Geneva told herself. That's all it was about. When they were out of earshot, she said, "Reporters hate the old just friends line."

"Probably. But we are friends," he said.

Were they? she wondered. She didn't sense tension from him but wouldn't let herself trust that feeling. "Still, with our history, and insatiable media curiosity, denials are guaranteed to fire up speculation and put the Sullivan name in print. Way to go, Michael."

"Thank you." He noted the group just entering the room. "Teri and Dex are here with his family."

Geneva had met them—Dex's father Frank, mother Elaine and younger siblings Carla and Jim. The family had practically adopted Michael and Teri after the loss of their parents. And she was the woman they'd watched leave Michael at the altar. Probably they knew she'd planned this shindig, but seeing her wouldn't get their evening off to a pleasant start.

"I'm going to check last minute details," she said to him.

"Okay." He stared at her for several moments, before turning away.

Then he joined the others who welcomed him with hugs, kisses, smiles and laughter. Geneva felt something hollow widen inside her, something cold, dark, empty. She recognized it as envy. He and Teri had suffered a great tragedy and she couldn't imagine how they'd felt. But they'd gained another family.

She'd never felt that sense of belonging even once. Maybe she just didn't know how to belong. To anyone.

Behind the scenes, Geneva conferred with the wait staff for a refresher course in the server boot camp she'd put them through. When she returned, the banquet room was filled with guests and she stood in the background to observe. She and Michael never had an engagement party. He'd wanted to get married as soon as possible, what with her being pregnant. Then she'd lost the baby.

When she noticed Teri coming toward her, she forced a smile and braced herself.

"Geneva, I was looking for you."

They had a truce, fragile but so far holding up.

"Here I am," she answered. Absolutely not hiding was what she'd wanted to say. Just standing in this shadowy back corner ready to spring into action if there were unexpected surprises. "Beautiful dress. You look fabulous."

The sapphire-blue satin gown clung to every curve and set off Teri's dark hair and eyes. "Thanks. So do you."

"Nice of you to say so." Geneva waited. "Did you need something?"

The other woman looked uncomfortable. "Yeah. To say thanks."

"Not necessary. Your brother said spare no expense. I didn't."

"Everything's perfect. You've obviously worked very hard and I want you to know how much Dex and I appreciate it."

Geneva heard something in the other woman's voice and looked closer. Hostility she always expected, although they were working up to tolerance. She didn't see either in Teri at the moment. There was tension. Something about Teri's eyes said she was a bride-to-be who felt the strain of a wedding commitment. If anyone could recognize the signs, it was Geneva.

"Teri? Are you okay?"

"Fine. Maybe a little tired. Dex and I have been working hard. Now with his family in town, the hours are stretched pretty thin."

"If anyone knows the pressures of getting married, it's me."

"That's right." Teri's forehead creased in thought. "Now that I think about it, I remember the rehearsal dinner the night before your wedding."

"That was a difficult time. I wasn't sleeping," Geneva admitted. "I had one nerve left and everyone was getting on it. I was strung so tight, if that nerve had snapped, it would have put out someone's eye."

Teri didn't smile. "You and I talked in the ladies' room. You told me you were having doubts."

Big time. And she'd picked a hell of a time to voice

them. "I'm sorry, Teri. I needed to talk to someone, but I shouldn't have bothered you. You're Michael's sister."

"I was also your friend. And your maid of honor."

"There was wine," Geneva recalled. "It loosened my tongue. Not in a good way."

"You said you were afraid Michael didn't love you."

As it turned out, she'd been right. "I was having anxiety issues."

"And I said the equivalent of snap out of it."

"But you said it with a great deal of charm." Geneva was trying to coax a smile.

"I had all the sensitivity of a water buffalo. And the next day we all found out how much I'd helped you. Well, now the sling-back pump is on the other foot. I wonder if the Fates punish advice-challenged maids of honor."

Geneva laughed. "Don't feel like the Typhoid Mary of matrimony. My problems had nothing to do with what you said. Your situation is different. You and Dex have known each other a long time."

"I know." The lines of worry in her forehead didn't smooth out.

"You're going to be very happy. Go have fun. That's an order from your event planner."

Teri nodded, then gave her an impulsive hug. "Thanks again for your hard work."

Coming from Michael's sister, the gesture meant a lot. But Geneva kept it to herself that planning this party had been the easy part. Seeing Teri's brother and keeping him informed about the details had been the real challenge. But tonight she didn't have to see him, at least not up close and personal. She would make sure everything continued to run smoothly, and stay in the background while she did. The media had their photo op with her and Michael, but the rest of the night wasn't about the past. It was about a bright future for Teri and Dex.

Although she wasn't the only one revisiting the past, she realized later when Frank Smith stood up and tapped on a glass for attention. Dex's father was tall, distinguished and still handsome, a preview of what his son would look like as an older man.

He cleared his throat. "I'd like to thank Michael Sullivan for this party. And for raising a special girl like Teri."

People clapped and whistled and he held up his hands for quiet. "Michael's mother and father were good friends to Elaine and me. God took them from us too soon. We stood by in case we were needed, but Michael held it all together. He graduated college while he was working and raising his sister. She's a fine young woman and my son is a lucky man. So tonight as we celebrate their engagement, I want to share something Teri and Michael's mother once said. Life isn't measured by the number of breaths we take, but by the moments that take our breath away. She's looking down from heaven tonight and wishing you both a lifetime of breathless moments."

Geneva was an emotional wreck and glad to be standing in the shadows as tears blurred her eyes. It must have been incredibly difficult for Michael— doing what he did while still grieving for his parents. And becoming amazingly successful while doing all of the above. He was an extraordinary man. The more she got to know him again, the more she realized it.

He was the last to toast the couple. When Teri hugged him, the spontaneous affection practically put Geneva in the blubbering idiot category. Because she was the planner, Geneva knew the toasts were pretty much the end of the evening, although the guests were invited to stay and party as long as they liked. But for her it was over and she almost made it out the door.

Michael stopped her. "Hey, Cinderella, it's not midnight. Got a pumpkin valet parked?"

"The hotel staff is standing by if anyone needs anything. My work here is done," she said lightly, hoping the subdued lighting hid the traces of tears still in her eyes.

"And spectacular work it was. You've set a high bar for yourself. This is going to be a tough act to follow."

His voice was teasing, but tell that to her swirling emotions. She'd been fighting tears and was afraid his praise would push her over the edge. Her vulnerability was showing and this was no time to face Michael. "I'm glad you're happy with everything. Good night."

He put a hand on her arm. "What is it, Geneva? Are you crying?"

"Of course not," she said, sniffling. "I'm a professional. A rock. Nerves of steel. There's no crying in events planning."

He handed her his handkerchief. "If you say so."

"Darn right," she said, dabbing at her eyes. Black mascara streaked the pristine cloth. "Sorry."

With a knuckle, he nudged her chin up and studied her face. "Why are you sad?"

"Who says I'm sad? Haven't you ever heard the expression tears of joy?"

"Yes. And I figured I had a fifty-fifty chance with that guess. I can never tell the difference. But you didn't answer the question. Which is it? Happy or sad?"

She shrugged. "I'm not sure."

"Then I have no idea how to respond appropriately."

"Maybe it's a little of both," she said, pleased and a little surprised he felt inclined to bother with her emotions at all. "I was just imagining how awful, how hard it must have been to lose your parents."

He frowned and slid his hands into his pockets. "Yeah. It was."

"But you and Teri had the Smiths. And each other. That must have helped. To have people to count on."

"Dex's family are salt of the earth—" He stopped and met her gaze. "Must have helped? That sounded like a personal aside. You had your parents."

"Not so much." She pulled at the handkerchief in her hands. "They fought over my custody for a long time before my mother won. After a while, she got tired of being a responsible single mom."

"What happened?"

"She dumped me on my grandmother while she dated. Eventually both my parents remarried and started new families. I stayed where I was."

"You didn't go to live with your mother?" Anger vibrated in his voice.

"We talked it over. But the conversation was more her telling me what I wanted. I didn't want to rock the boat. I wanted to stay where I was—at my school with my friends. I wanted the best possible start for her and my stepfather."

"Son of a bitch—"

The anger in his tone was raw and deep and she wished she could go there, too. She simply felt miserable and humiliated, especially when she saw the pity in his eyes. The last thing she wanted was Michael Sullivan feeling sorry for her. If only she could take back all the wretched details she'd revealed about her childhood. With her defenses down, she should have kept going when he stopped her from leaving. Since she hadn't had a drop of alcohol, this time she couldn't even blame it on the wine.

She plastered a carefree smile on her face. "Isn't it funny how weddings bring out emotions?" She let her gaze roam to the people beyond him. "Speaking of which, you should go back to your guests. Good night, Michael."

"No, you don't." He stopped her again with a hand on her arm. "I don't think I've ever seen someone more in need of a hug than you."

Before she could stop him, he drew her into his arms and settled her against the solid length of him. The strength and warmth and support melted her resistance like an ice cube in the hot sun. She couldn't resist resting her cheek on his chest and savoring the steady, strong beat of his heart.

She hadn't wanted his pity, but as he'd said, when life gives you lemons… Unfortunately one had to take the sour with the sweet.

She let out one long sigh, then pulled away and smiled up at him. "This is your party, Michael. Yours and Teri's and Dex's. The last thing I want to do is rain on your parade. Literally," she said lightly. "Go be with everyone."

"Come with me."

She shook her head. "No. Go have fun. You deserve it."

This time she was glad he let her go before she did something else she'd regret.

"So, what do you think about marrying your knight in shining armor at the Excalibur?"

Geneva was in the back of Michael's limousine with him and Teri sitting across from her. After touring three possible sites on the Las Vegas strip for her wedding, they were back at the Sullivan Hotel where Teri worked. Geneva was trying, without much success, to get a thumbs-up from the skittish bride. A week ago at the engagement party, she'd felt something was wrong with Teri, now she was sure of it.

Teri tapped her lip. "The idea of Dex as Lancelot is very romantic, but I don't think it's us." She looked at both of them. "You are aware that King Arthur and Guinevere's story resolved tragically and she ended up in a convent?"

"I can see the appeal," Michael said wryly.

"That's mean, Michael."

"Okay, you two," Geneva intervened. "Peace and love." She scratched Excalibur off her list. "For what it's worth, I liked the HMS Britannia at Treasure Island. The pirates were fun."

Teri frowned. "I don't think Dex is the swash and buckle type. He's a little shy. The rescuing me portion of the vows would make him freeze up."

"Not if you were in real danger," Michael volunteered. "And that could be arranged."

"Michael—" Geneva glared at him.

"If this wedding is going to happen on schedule, you need to pick a place so the invitations can go out."

"I'm trying." There was an edge to Teri's voice that could cut glass.

"Don't pressure her, Michael. When it's right, she'll know."

"Thank you, Geneva." Teri shot her brother a triumphant look.

"The Venetian had a couple of different ideas that might work." Geneva looked at her notes, then stopped when Teri's expression didn't soften with enthusiasm.

The bride-to-be folded her arms over her chest. "I don't know."

"I can check out a ceremony at Paris. We can't go to the Eiffel Tower in the most romantic city in the world, but there's a darn good imitation right here in our own backyard."

When Teri shrugged noncommittally, Michael frowned. "I vote for a wedding on the USS Enterprise at the Hilton. Your witnesses can be Klingons."

The situation was deteriorating rapidly and Geneva was at a loss. Something was bothering Teri and until that was resolved, no decision would be forthcoming. Geneva had a feeling the bride was having doubts, which was probably normal, even for the well-adjusted, average bride.

In Geneva's case, it had been more than nerves. She'd had solid reasons for the way she'd felt. She hadn't known Michael more than a few months. But her worst mistake was in not dealing with her misgivings before things went so far. Now she had to live with the regrets about Michael. And the man had hugged her, for God's sake, fueling this *thing* for him that just wouldn't quit.

Teri opened the limo door and slid out. "You're no help, Michael. This is my wedding and I want it to be perfect. Thank goodness for Geneva. Next time we go looking, you can't come."

After the door slammed, Michael looked like a man at his wit's end. "I've known her from birth and been her guardian since she was ten. We're probably closer than most siblings. But at this moment, I don't know her at all."

"She's never been engaged before."

"So?" He shook his head. "She loves him. He loves her. A wedding is the next logical step."

"Are you channeling the Star Trek Experience? You sound like Spock."

Michael grinned. "I like him. No emotion to muck up logical thinking."

Geneva wondered where he'd stashed the sensitive man who'd hugged her. This was the Michael who had asked her to marry him when she was pregnant. Logical. Unemotional. The right thing. This was the man who'd doused her doubts with kerosene.

"Michael, you're going to have to deal with the fact that by definition, your sister is female and therefore emotional. And the stress she's under right now is going to exacerbate her emotionalness."

One dark eyebrow rose. "Is that a word?"

"Did you get my drift?"

"Yes."

"Then it's a word."

"So you're saying this is a chick thing?"

Geneva glared at him. "I'm saying she's not like you. And even if she were, sharing chromosomes wouldn't give you the code to decipher what's going through her mind. If that were the case, I'd have a clue why my parents got married in the first place. I'd know what makes them tick."

"You're mixing metaphors or something," he said, amusement flashing briefly in his eyes.

"The point is, all I ever saw was the part of their marriage where they fought, then tried to hurt each other more. I thought everyone lived that way."

"That must have been very difficult for you."

"It was. I read a lot when I was a kid," she admitted. "Books were a haven for me, an escape from the fighting and yelling and wounding with words."

"What did you read?" he asked.

"Does it matter?"

"Yes."

She sighed. "I read fairy tales. I loved the endings, the happily-ever-after. I wanted that so much. But it never happened. When my parents were within spitting distance of each other, you could cut the tension with a dull butter knife. I started having stomach problems and for a while they thought it might be an ulcer."

"Jeez, Geneva—" He slid forward on the seat and met her gaze, his own dark with intensity. "I didn't know."

"How could you? I never said anything."

"I wish you had. It explains a lot."

A lot, but not everything, she thought. It just explained her fear and reluctance. It explained why she felt marriage was quicksand. Taking vows was the step that sucked you in before things turned really unpleasant.

Her grandmother had said her parents fell in love at first sight. Geneva had thought that so romantic, before all hell broke loose. To make matters worse, the moment she'd laid eyes on Michael, she'd wanted him. She still did. It was the tension, bitterness and harsh words she could do without, and that's what would have happened.

She didn't blame him for being angry about the way she'd called off the wedding. But after he'd had time to calm down and think straight, she thought he'd call her. Wouldn't he have contacted her if he'd really loved her?

He continued to stare at her. "We need to work on our communication."

"You're right." She tucked her notes into her brief-case. "But now I have work to do."

"That's not what I meant. There's nothing wrong with our business information flow."

"Then we're fine."

He looked baffled as he shook his head. "We were going to get married."

Pain she'd pushed into a protective bubble a year

ago pushed and prodded and threatened to escape. "Not a newsflash, boss. What's your point?"

"I don't have a point. Questions are something else."

A year ago she wouldn't have asked. But she'd faced a lot since then. What doesn't kill you makes you stronger and Michael Sullivan didn't intimidate her now.

"Like what questions for instance?" she asked.

"For instance," he said, "why are there so many things we didn't know about each other?"

Let me count the whys, she thought. His demanding career. And hers. The baby and losing her. Before that, there was the overpowering attraction that pushed out everything else except the need to be together. Bringing up the specifics would be like slicing open her heart, guaranteeing that it would never work again.

Geneva settled for a more general truth.

She met his gaze and the intensity that made him such a compelling and unforgettable man. "It all happened so fast."

"But still—" Confusion darkened his eyes as he ran a hand through his hair.

"Still," she said more gently. "Learning things about each other takes time. Possibly a lifetime."

A muscle worked in his jaw as he stared out the smoky glass window of the limo. "Sometimes you don't get a lifetime."

Geneva knew he was talking about his parents.

"They made a life together. They never had to wonder what might have been."

"Yeah."

"And in my opinion before Teri blows her chance for what could be, you need to talk to her and find out what's up."

CHAPTER SIX

MICHAEL didn't need anyone to tell him that he had to talk to Teri. He'd raised her.

After instructing his driver to take Geneva back to her office at the other hotel, he watched the big car glide smoothly into traffic on Las Vegas Boulevard. He let out a long breath when she was gone.

Sometimes you don't get a lifetime.

What had made him say that? His parents were dead and that was a tragedy. But he'd moved through all the stages of grief, from anger to acceptance. And he'd done the same when Geneva left him. He'd moved forward with his fury as a shield. The more he got to know about Geneva, the faster that shield was failing, something he would deal with later. Right now he needed to find out what was going on with his sister.

He turned and walked briskly into the lobby, then took the elevator to the executive offices. Teri's was at the end of the hall, across from Dex's, each situated on a corner of the building with floor to ceiling windows on two sides.

Michael stalked into Teri's office with its paintings of ocean scenes, a Waterford crystal vase filled with fresh flowers on her desk and shelves with her collection of Lladro. She liked chick things around; he preferred Spartan and serviceable. Another difference in their DNA.

"What the hell is wrong with you?" he asked, standing in front of her desk.

She looked up and her dark eyes took on a defiant glare. "I'm perfectly fine, thank you very much. Now I've got work to do. Not that your barging in here hasn't been really fun."

He ran his fingers through his hair. "Let's start over."

"What's this 'us' stuff? I didn't start anything."

"Okay. *I'll* start over. You're not yourself."

Teri tossed her pen on top of the papers. "Then who am I?"

"Not the decisive sister I know and love."

She blinked, then looked away. "What was your first clue?"

"Teri Sullivan wouldn't have this much trouble deciding where to have a wedding if there wasn't something bugging her big time."

"Sometimes I hate that you know me so well."

"What's wrong?" His voice gentled when she turned bleak eyes on him.

"I'm having doubts about getting married."

"I see." That wasn't a huge surprise. Michael rested a hip on the corner of her desk. "What kind of doubts?"

"So many doubts, so little time."

"Take as much time as you need. This is important."

"Okay." She let out a long breath. "Dex is a wonderful man. But is he right for me? Did I just say yes to his proposal because we've known each other forever? Because he's your best friend and you approve and want us together? Or am I really in love with him?"

"Only you can answer that."

"That's the problem." She threw up her hands. "I can't answer it. We were drifting through life happy as two clams until he had to go and screw it up by asking me to marry him."

"I thought—and let me quote you—'he went down on one knee. It was so romantic.'"

"But marriage isn't romance," she retorted. "It's a contract with the state."

"Ah. So you have issues about making a serious and legal commitment for the rest of your life."

"Yes!" She leaned back in her chair. "I didn't think you'd understand."

"Of course I do. Everyone has qualms. It's normal."

"Did you?" she asked.

"I remember being nervous. With good reason, as it turned out. Hindsight is twenty-twenty."

"There's a lot of that going around."

"What does that mean?" he asked sharply. She had a sheepish expression on her face, the way she used to look when she was a little girl trying to hide something.

"The night before your wedding, Geneva talked to me about her doubts."

Geneva's recent revelations had clued him in to how many doubts she must have had, but she'd never said a word to him.

"What did she tell you?"

"I don't remember specifically," Teri answered. "In general she said that she was afraid the two of you were making a mistake."

"What did you say?"

She didn't quite look him in the eye. "Something along the lines of suck it up. Snap out of it. Get over it."

"Teri—"

She held her hand up. "Not quite those words."

"Did she say anything about her mother and father?"

"Not that I recall. Why?"

He sighed. "Apparently they were a cautionary tale about the pitfalls of parenting and matrimony."

"You didn't know?"

"That she went through hell as a kid? Not until recently." He filled Teri in on what Geneva had told him about being an innocent victim in her parents' bad marriage and worse divorce. "When they couldn't use her anymore, they dumped her on her grandmother."

"Oh, Michael—" She looked stunned. "I can't even imagine."

"Yeah."

"Our parents were taken suddenly and no one had a choice." She met his gaze. "But think about what it must have been like for Geneva."

"You mean knowing both your father and mother were alive and well somewhere and neither of them wanted you?" Anger simmered through him. "I get it."

"I wish I'd known," Teri admitted.

"Join the club." He stood and walked over to the window, looking out on the street's bumper-to-bumper traffic. The tourists were elbow to elbow, walking up and down Las Vegas Boulevard.

"I feel horrible, Michael. Geneva tried to talk to me and I blew her off. I said something to the effect that the two of you couldn't be wrong because my big brother always does the right thing."

"Great." He turned back to her and slid his hands in his pockets.

"Michael?" Her eyes narrowed.

"Did she say anything to that?"

Teri shook her head. "Actually she got a funny look on her face. Like the wind shifted and she'd just gotten a whiff of the pig farm."

"Damn it—"

She frowned. "What's wrong, Michael?"

What wasn't wrong? Did Geneva's troubled childhood make a difference now? He hoped not. She'd walked out on him once. It would be worse than stupid to willingly lower his shield and give her another shot at him. It would make him a fool.

"It's my problem. I came here to talk about you and Dex."

"I'd rather talk about you." Teri looked miserable.

"If you feel that way," he said, "you might want to think about not going through with the wedding."

"But we had the engagement party. His parents are so happy. And you're happy. And the publicity. For Sullivan Towers." Shadows swirled in her eyes as she met his gaze. "Michael—"

"None of that matters if you're not happy. The choice you make should come from the heart. Don't get me wrong. I like you and Dex together. And from a purely business standpoint, the publicity is a good thing. But if there's the slightest doubt in your mind, all the right things in the world aren't enough reason to get married—"

"What, Michael? You look like you just swallowed bad sushi."

"I wish." This was déjà vu all over again. "Everything I just said to you is practically a direct quote from Geneva when she told a chapel full of people why she couldn't go through with the wedding."

"Really?" Teri's eyes widened.

"The content of her message isn't something I'm likely to forget."

"There's a lot of wisdom in what she said."

He started pacing in front of Teri's desk. "And she didn't run away. She faced everyone."

"That took a lot of guts," Teri commented.

No kidding. She'd taken responsibility for not taking responsibility sooner. And just like that, genuine respect and admiration for Geneva pushed out his lingering anger.

Teri picked up her pen and ran it through her fingers. "We've been pretty judgmental. At least I gave her an apology of sorts."

"You did? When?"

"At the engagement party. She noticed that I was acting weird and asked why. All of these feelings about Dex stirred up a lot of stuff. Including memories about you and Geneva and the night of your rehearsal dinner." Teri was obviously putting herself in Geneva's shoes.

"What did she say when you apologized?"

Teri grinned, then shrugged. "Typical Geneva. Gracious and funny."

That was his Geneva. No. Not his. The anger had evaporated, but that didn't mean he'd go another round with her.

Although now that he was looking back without resentment, he saw their situation from a different perspective. Things between them *had* happened fast. He hadn't been able to slow himself down because she was gracious, fun, funny, smart and sexy. And so beautiful.

He missed his anger; he wanted it back. To hide behind. To help him forget the good stuff. Because if he didn't, he'd remember he needed her, and that would lead to wanting a lifetime with her. No one knew better than he did that it could all be snatched away in a heartbeat.

Geneva sighed when she realized she'd been staring at her computer screen for at least five minutes and had no idea what she'd intended to do. All she could see was the pity in Michael's eyes. Every time she saw him, it seemed she was revealing something else about her life. He was probably thanking his lucky stars that she'd called off the wedding. He'd dodged a major catastrophe because she was damaged, dysfunctional and a complete emotional wreck.

That changed right now.

She was going to forget about the past. It had shaped who she was but she wouldn't let it define her. From now on, when she spent time with Michael Sullivan, there would be no painful, personal disclosures or the poor man would probably run screaming from the room—or the limo—as the case might be.

Geneva resolved to be all business all the time and she had some very pressing business—the events surrounding the first public sales release of Sullivan Towers followed by Teri Sullivan's wedding. Although event number two was shaky. Which reminded her— she was worried about Teri. She was trying to decide whether or not to call Teri when she noticed Michael in the doorway to her office.

"Hi."

Geneva's hands started to shake. "Hi, yourself. I was just thinking about you."

"Isn't it handy that I showed up?"

She wasn't sure how to answer that and rested her forearms on her desk as she studied him. There was something different about him but she couldn't put her finger on the change.

"Was it good?" he asked.

She blinked, drawing a blank about his meaning. "What?"

"The things you were thinking about me."

"Oh." Good? Not from her perspective. But telling him she didn't plan to dump on him anymore would violate the spirit of the directive she'd just given herself, which was not to get personal the next time she saw him. She just hadn't known it would be so soon. But the gleam in his eyes said he was waiting for an answer. "Why do I get the feeling you're fishing for compliments?"

"Because I am."

"Well, then—" How did she get out of this one? Bob and weave? Evasive maneuvers? "What was the question again?"

"Why were you thinking about me?"

She'd go with either being a glutton for punishment or certifiably insane, because thinking about

Michael wasn't smart. He wasn't going to cut her any slack. So it was time to deflect the subject.

"Let me put a finer point on it. Technically I was wondering how your talk with Teri went."

He moved into the room and sat in one of the chairs on the other side of her desk. Interesting. Normally he moved right into her space and effortlessly stirred up her disobedient hormones. It was darned annoying that he'd kept his distance and her hormones were still going bonkers.

"How did the talk go?" he said absently. "It was certainly different from the talk I had with her about where babies come from."

"That tells me nothing," she informed him.

"I'm still assessing damage."

Geneva couldn't keep up with him. His playful, flirtatious mood had turned enigmatic. She decided to be more specific. "What did Teri say?"

"She's having doubts about getting married."

"I see."

"She's not sure if she's in love with Dex or if she agreed because everyone around her thinks it's a good idea."

"I was afraid of that," Geneva admitted.

"Not surprised?" His smile was fleeting. "I suppose her recent behavior was as obvious as all the neon on Las Vegas Boulevard."

"I guess," she agreed. "Being the queen of matrimonial misgivings, I spotted the clues right away."

As he met her gaze, he leaned forward and rested his elbows on his knees. "Why didn't you tell me?"

"About Teri? It wasn't any of my business."

"No," he said. "About your doubts."

No way, she thought. Not talking about this. Because her major doubt had been whether or not he loved her. Now she knew he hadn't. "The more important question is whether or not you want me to scrap the wedding plans?"

"Just put things on hold."

"Okay." She nodded. "No firm decisions have been made, so no harm done. Now, about the—"

"About us," he interrupted. Something hot flickered in his eyes, something that sizzled and smoldered. "I know things moved fast, but you could have told me anything."

"That's good to know." She smiled, then glanced away as her pulse skipped. Aside from keeping discussions strictly business, the bigger challenge was getting the message from her brain to her body that it wasn't safe to respond to his masculinity. Glancing through her calendar she said, "I think I've got a phone appointment scheduled with Melina St. George—"

"Who?"

"She's a chef. In New York. We were going to discuss possible menus." She tapped her lip. "I'll leave it for now. Teri can let me know what she wants me to do."

He nodded. "Talking about the problem might take the edge off her stress."

"I agree. Was there anything else? If not I have work—"

"What's with you?" His voice dropped into the irritated range.

"I could ask you the same thing. I'm just trying to be a productive employee. What's your excuse?"

"Work is the last thing I want to talk about."

Uh-oh. "Then that rules out everything but personal stuff and I don't want to go there. Aren't you getting tired of hearing 'poor Geneva' stories? Because I'm sure getting tired of telling them."

He slid his fingers into his pockets. "If you'd told me about your parents and the divorce before the wedding, I'd have understood. I could have—"

"What?" she asked, emotions bubbling through her, pressing against her chest. She clasped her hands together and rested them on the desk. "I'll admit that I was terrified of repeating my parents' mistakes. Their marriage was the only blueprint I had and it was so terribly flawed. How could I do it better?" She sighed. "But my timing was really bad. And there's no way you would have understood, no matter what you think now."

"Now I think that any time the media mentions Michael Sullivan, the story will include a footnote about being left at the altar by gorgeous Geneva Porter."

Her heart beat erratically as she stared at the

humor in his eyes and realized any lingering bitterness was gone. It felt as if the invisible walls between them had tumbled down and that was bad.

"For what it's worth, the decision to call off the wedding was very difficult for me." For so many reasons. The baby, for one thing, she thought. And Michael, the spell he cast over her.

He moved forward and leaned a hip against her desk. "I have a pretty good idea how hard it was for you to stand up in front of all those people."

Was that respect in his expression? She never thought Michael would look at her that way. Half of her wanted to do the dance of joy. The other half didn't believe him. It was safest to go with the other half.

She blew out a long breath. "I told myself that facing everyone was the lesser of two evils."

"Marriage to me would be evil?" It wasn't clear whether his tone reflected amusement or offense.

"It is if it would make both of us unhappy."

"You don't know that," he said, defensively.

"Neither do you. And that's the point. You must have had some doubts, too."

"Why do you say that?"

"Because you let me walk away."

"It's what you wanted."

"I called off the wedding and tried to apologize to you. You let me go. You never once said let's talk about it. Or you hated my guts. Or go to hell. There was just nothing. You never looked back. Silence speaks volumes and yours said you agreed with my decision." The catch in her voice made a mockery of her decision not to get personal.

"I'm talking about it now."

"It's too late, Michael."

"You're wrong. I—"

"What?"

He glanced at his watch and frowned. "I can't talk now. I have a meeting with the contractors." Then he walked to the door. "We'll talk later."

She'd already talked too much. She'd never meant to tell him any of her feelings and the stuff about her childhood was small potatoes compared to what she'd just revealed.

Talk was cheap, but the cost in heartache could be very high.

CHAPTER SEVEN

MICHAEL found it hard to concentrate. He found that a lot when he was with Geneva. But it was almost 7:00 p.m. and she was sitting stiffly in his office, a welcome addition to one of the leather chairs in front of his desk. She was bringing him up to speed on all the hotel's upcoming events. At the moment, he was far more interested in her dimples. And her mouth.

It had been a couple of weeks since that day she'd nailed him with the truth. He'd had doubts about marriage and commitment. But mostly he hadn't wanted to need her. If he was being honest, once the shock of her leaving had worn off, he'd been relieved about her calling off the wedding. But she was wrong about him not looking back. The problem was he'd weighed his pride against public rejection and pride had won.

At least until recently when he'd learned more about her.

Now—Hell, now he'd only admit to fascination bordering on obsession for her extraordinary legs.

"After the CineVegas Film Festival, we've got the gizmos and gadgets guys—"

"Who?" It had taken some doing to distract him from wanting to trace the depth of her dimples, but that remark got his attention.

"You know—" She glanced at her notes. "The geeks and nerds who bring the latest inventions for the electronics show. It's like watching the Sci-fi channel."

"Because they look like aliens?" he asked.

"No. Because some of their inventions are so futuristic."

"I take it you're not looking forward to geeks and nerds on the loose."

"I'm sure they're lovely people," she said, her tone smacking of political correctness. "All right." She sighed. "I hate technology."

"Miss Porter, I'm shocked and appalled."

"Sad but true. It's my tragic flaw. My dark little secret. Computers are a necessary evil." She tapped her pen on the legal pad in her lap to punctuate her words. "But make no mistake—they *are* evil."

"An invention of the devil."

"Actually the geeks and nerds are responsible. And just when I think I'm marginally proficient, they go and come up with some new gizmo that's *supposed* to make things easier. So just who are they trying to help?"

For him this was new. He found her completely charming and practically irresistible. Correction: maybe not new, but simply not overshadowed by the bad stuff. The question was what to do about it. They'd been down this road before. Granted, they'd traveled at speeds a NASCAR champion would envy. This time they were loaded down with emotional baggage.

What hadn't changed was the way he wanted her. But where were they going? And did he want to take the journey?

Michael stood and came around the desk, then rested a hip against it. He was so close he could smell the sweet scent of her perfume and feel the warmth of her skin. So close he watched the pulse in her neck jump and go wild.

"So let me get this straight. In your opinion, the gizmos and gadgets guys are the spawn of Satan?"

"Yes." She shifted uneasily under his gaze.

"I guess you just have to chalk it up to everyone has their talents and yours run along artistic lines."

She frowned. "Is that a don't-worry-your-little-head remark?"

"Absolutely not," he promised.

"Okay. Just asking. The thing is, the technology guys are loyal customers and about five hundred will be checking in at the same time. That will be a challenge. Along with fitting them and all their gadgets into the largest space available in the hotel. We're going to have to open the divider and expand the banquet room to provide an area large enough to display their advanced electronic devices of torture."

"What about electrical access?"

"I know when I'm in over my head. I'm working with the engineering staff. We'll need industrial strength extension cords, but the guys are handling that."

"Okay." He nodded. "What about Sullivan Towers? The grand opening is about six weeks away."

"As you know, we're making it a weekend event. Invitations have been sent out to everyone on the priority list. I'm pulling out all the stops for a reception Friday night. Saturday we'll have a media heavy ribbon cutting ceremony for the sales office and your real estate professionals will do an elaborate presentation. They'll unveil the different floor plans and talk about preconstruction pricing."

"Right."

"We'll have random drawings for a weekend at the hotel. A round of golf at the country club. Massage and spa packages."

"The freebies that bring people out."

"Celebrity type people," she agreed. She checked her notes. "We've had a very positive response."

"Everything's on track?"

"Yes." She closed her file and stood, backing up several steps. "So I guess that's all."

When business was done so were they? As he stared at her full lips, he realized he'd had enough business for one day and a little pleasure now couldn't hurt.

"I'm not quite finished," he said.

"Oh?"

"Have you talked to Teri?"

She nodded. "I know the wedding is on. Apparently Dex demanded to know what was wrong and they talked things through—"

"Unlike us."

"Right." She folded her arms over her chest, the file in front like a barrier. "She's decided on a place— the wedding chapel at Lake Las Vegas."

"Elegant. Upscale. Nice," he said, studying her tempting lips.

"Yes. Now we can proceed with food, flowers and invitations."

"I want to see the invitation list after you get it from my sister."

"Right. For business contacts. That could make for a long guest list."

"Like ours," he remembered.

"There were a lot of people there," she agreed. "Heaven forbid anyone important should have missed my embarrassing little speech. My preference would have been a ceremony with you, me and the Klingons—um, I mean witnesses."

"You didn't want a big wedding?" He was surprised.

She shook her head. "I'd have preferred small and intimate."

Imagine that. An events planner who wanted a nonevent. Again he had to ask, "Why didn't you tell me?"

She shrugged. "Because you're Michael Sullivan."

"So?"

She tilted her head, studying him. "You're charismatic, larger-than-life. It was easy to get swept away. Who can say no to you?"

She could, he thought. "It was your wedding, too."

She gripped the back of the chair she kept between them. "Believe me, I learned how foolish it is not to be straightforward. I'll never again make the mistake of keeping my feelings to myself."

He tried to remember back. Had she given him a clue? He wouldn't deny he'd gotten used to having his orders carried out without question. "I'd like to think I'd have listened and understood. But I can't guarantee it."

She smiled, but there was sadness in her eyes. "That's nice of you to say, Michael."

Although she stood tall, he towered over her. Still, she looked him straight in the eye, unbending, direct. She'd admitted a mistake, faced it and gained wisdom. She was all the stronger for the ordeal. She was silk and steel.

Her healthy, toned body wasn't the only difference in her, Michael realized. She'd become a confident woman, sure of herself. Self-assurance looked good on her.

Really good.

Before the idea went through a proper thought process, the words were coming out of his mouth. "It's getting late and I haven't had dinner. Will you join me?"

Wide eyes grew even wider. "Do you really think that would be wise?"

Probably not. But since when did a guy fall back on wisdom when he had more testosterone than common sense? "Do you always answer a question with a question?" he asked.

"Do you?" Her full lips curved up.

God, he wanted her. "Yes or no, Geneva?" He all but growled the words.

"How about thank you, no?" She backed away. "I've got work to do. Good night, Michael."

He let out a long breath and folded his arms over his chest as he started to go after her. At the doorway, he stopped himself. What was it about Geneva that made him come back for more rejection?

The answer was simple. He wanted her and he intended to have her. Anticipation hummed through him when he realized the differences in her wouldn't make it easy.

So he had the answer to his question: he was taking the journey again. Not the same journey. This time around he knew better than to let his emotions get in the way.

* * *

When had she started to anticipate seeing Michael? Geneva decided she should find a way to shut down whatever part of her was half expecting Michael to appear in her office doorway, lounge there, then invite her to dinner. What woman in her right mind turns down a dinner invitation from Michael Sullivan? *The* Michael Sullivan.

Because she'd had something better to do? She held her hands out in front of her, palms up as if weighing her alternatives.

"Dinner with a handsome, sexy, funny, man. Also fabulously wealthy." She lifted one palm. "Or a frozen, albeit low calorie entrée in a beautiful, cozy, albeit lonely mortgaged-to-the-hilt condo." She raised the other hand, to just below the first. "Geneva, you're definitely not in your right mind."

Anyone who'd heard her dilemma would agree. And this wasn't the first time she'd regretted not accepting Michael's invitation.

The way he'd looked at her… Her breath caught and her heart tilted, remembering he'd looked as if he wanted to devour her and make her love every second. But she couldn't be sure she could trust her instincts—or him, for that matter. Besides, they'd had their shot, and it had been a disaster. A smart girl wouldn't go there again and Geneva considered herself pretty smart.

Just then her phone rang and she picked it up. "Geneva Porter."

"Geneva, it's Peter."

He was the manager of Pinnacle, the premier restaurant at the hotel. She'd worked with him often on special events. "What can I do for you?"

"Would you mind coming up here for a minute?"

Admittedly she had her hands full of other Sullivan projects, but the hotel always had something going on. Off the top of her head, she couldn't remember if there was anything pending with Peter. "Is there a problem?"

"No crisis. I could just use your help with something."

"I'll be right there."

Geneva took the elevator down to the lobby where she got into another one, a private car, that was the only way to reach Pinnacle on the top floor. When the doors opened it was like walking into another world. Subdued lighting, dark wood and floor-to-ceiling windows with a view of the neon skyline of Vegas. No jeans and T-shirts here. Coat and tie for the men—an opportunity for the ladies to wear that fancy after-five dress.

She stood by the windows for a moment, always enjoying the sight of the signature green glow of the MGM Grand Hotel. The light on top of Luxor's Pyramid lasered the inky blackness of the sky. Was it really black? she wondered. Or did it only look that way in contrast to the breathtaking glitter below? The sight never failed to stir her imagination. God, she loved it here, where the sky was the limit. Any conceivable indulgence. Instantaneous millionaires. It was the one place on the planet that instantly conjured possibilities. `

Then Michael was beside her.

"Hi." Her breath caught at the sight of him and for a moment or two she simply stared. Then she pulled herself together. "Whatever Peter wants must be bad if you're here. But he said there's no crisis. What's going on?"

"There's nothing wrong." He settled his hand at the small of her waist and guided her down the short corridor to the restaurant. "Come with me."

She couldn't think about anything but the warmth of Michael's palm searing through her silk blouse. She could feel the heat of each individual finger and her heart did that tilting thing again. He guided her through the restaurant, past the main room where tables were arranged two steps up on a sort of dais and surrounded by a half wall of frosted glass, topped with a brass handrail. The place was full of people and the hum of voices, the clatter of silverware and the musical tinkle of crystal.

But Michael kept her moving. She went along with him to one of the rooms off the main dining area used for larger private parties. Or smaller private parties, she thought, looking at the intimate table set for two. A fresh bouquet of flowers filled the air with perfume. Flickering flames from the tapers in crystal holders caught and reflected in the Waterford stemware and gold-trimmed china.

She stared up at him. "What is this?"

"I took the liberty of ordering dinner."

Liberties? Of course he took liberties. He was the great and powerful Michael Sullivan. Sort of like the Wizard of Oz, only rich and handsome. And he'd put stars in her eyes once upon a time. But she wasn't that spineless, mousy, or quietly desperate woman any longer. She was not easily intimidated by power and wealth. But if those were the only qualities in Michael that she found attractive, she wouldn't be in so much trouble. She needed to have a long talk with Peter and define the meaning of the word crisis.

She swallowed once as she stared at the romantic scene, then up at Michael, so handsome in his dark suit, snow-white shirt and red tie. Here she was again with choices staring her in the face. Romantic dinner? Or low-cal, frozen microwave entrée?

She desperately wanted to stay and that was why she couldn't.

"This is lovely, Michael. But—"

"Do you know how much I'm beginning to hate that word?"

"I'm sorry. It's just I have to—" She thought, frantically trying to come up with an excuse.

"Organize your sock drawer?" One dark eyebrow rose. "Clean out your refrigerator before the leftovers turn into fuzzy science projects gone wild?"

The old Geneva would have stuttered and stammered, then finally knuckled. The new and improved Geneva wasn't so easy. "I can't stay. If you'd given me some warning—"

"You'd have turned me down. If you have other plans—" He waited for a response.

She simply shrugged noncommittally, with all the dignity in the world. "I'm sorry."

"How about one glass of wine?" When she started to protest, he held up a hand. "Just to thank you for all the extra hours and your hard work. Teri and I are grateful."

He moved over to the table where a bottle of red wine was "breathing" and poured two glasses. "This is the Cabernet you like."

Against her better judgment, she took the glass he handed her. Apparently the old and new Genevas had something in common—they were both attracted to Michael Sullivan and had difficulty saying no to him. Did that make her a pillar of strength or just schizophrenic? She'd have a glass of wine, but she wouldn't sit down. She took a sip and the smooth, full-bodied liquid easily slid down her throat.

"This is good. How did you know I like it?"

"It's the one we drank that weekend we went to my house in Lake Tahoe."

Oh, yeah. *That* weekend. She remembered taking the company's corporate jet to the Reno airport where a limousine picked them up for a ride into the mountains and around the lake. His cabin—*some* cabin—about five thousand square feet of wood beams, glass windows and a view of the water from practically every room. A skylight in the master bedroom opened to a spectacular sky full of glittering stars.

She forced a thoughtful expression. "I think I remember."

"Do you remember falling in the lake?"

"You threw me in. As I recall it was after some heated discussion about wet T-shirts."

"I jumped in, too, so both our shirts would be wet."

"Yeah," she said wryly. "It was exactly the same thing."

He grinned. "Exactly."

"Good Lord that water was freezing."

His gaze dropped for a fraction of a second to her chest. "Not to me."

She wasn't sure whether it was the wine, the man or the memories, but suddenly she was way too warm. "Tahoe is a beautiful spot. A nice break from Vegas heat. Did you go much this summer?"

He shook his head. "I haven't been back at all."

What did that mean? Why hadn't he been back? Was it about her? Did she want it to be? Yes. And how selfish was that? Making a commitment probably wasn't in the cards for her and that wasn't fair to Michael. She wouldn't do this again.

"I guess you've been too busy with finalizing the hotel deal and now the Sullivan Towers project."

He shrugged. "I've had time."

Then why hadn't he gone? *Was* it about her? She leaned over and sniffed a particularly fragrant lily in one of the bouquets.

"The flowers are lovely."

"I know they're your favorites," he said.

"How?"

"You told me."

"When?" she asked.

"It was our first date." He sipped his wine, but his gaze never left hers. "I'd sent flowers and when I picked you up that night, you told me."

"Picked me up wearing a tuxedo." Her knees nearly buckled when he flashed a grin. "You said dinner. You never said it was formal."

"I liked your little sundress."

"That's not precisely accurate," she countered. "You liked taking it off."

"That's true." His grin filled with male satisfaction.

She finished the last of her wine and nervously twirled the empty glass. Technically it wasn't their first date because they never went out. They never made it to dinner.

"That was the night our baby was conceived." She met his gaze, her eyes burning with unshed tears.

She knew that was the night because neither of them had been prepared for the power of their passion. Carried away didn't do justice to what they'd felt. In their out-of-control need to be together, they hadn't been able to get their clothes off fast enough. And they'd made a baby. A girl.

It wasn't the last time they made love, just the only time they hadn't taken precautions.

"I know." His smile disappeared, replaced by a brooding look.

What was he thinking? On second thought, she didn't want to know. And the more time she spent with him, the more she wanted to throw caution to the wind, to take a chance. But Michael wasn't the sort of man to forget, let alone forgive.

She set her glass on the table. "I really have to go."

Pulling her dignity around her like a cloak, she left him. The tears gathering in her eyes didn't fall until she realized he let her go. Again. And she didn't want him to.

Again.

CHAPTER EIGHT

MICHAEL owned a limousine and had a driver on the payroll, but some days he preferred to do the driving himself and this was one of those days. He pulled the outrageously expensive two-seater Mercedes into Geneva's driveway, then glanced in his rearview mirror as he smoothed a hand over his windblown hair. Putting the top down had been irresistible. Otherwise, what was the point of having an outrageously expensive convertible?

Lately he'd begun to wonder about the point to life in general. He had everything money could buy, and a lot it couldn't: family, friends, a successful career and future goals. Yet, there was an emptiness.

He walked to Geneva's front door with its lovely, etched glass oval insert and knocked. Loud music pounded from inside. He removed his sunglasses and hung them in the vee of his tab front shirt, then peered through the glass when no one answered. He knew she was home, so he rang the bell. After a minute, he pulled out his cell phone. Her number was on his speed dial and he punched it.

When she picked up, he said, "Answer the front door."

A moment later the music was silenced and through the glass he saw her in the entryway, just before the door opened.

"Michael."

"Geneva."

In a town where fortunes were won or lost on a bluff, she was lucky to be an events planner because surprise was clear on her face. Obviously she hadn't been expecting anyone. The dust cloth in her hand was a clue. And she hadn't a speck of makeup on, her hair was carelessly pulled into a ponytail with tendrils fluttering around her face, and her short white shorts and thin-strapped neon-green tank top were casual, not professional. Although the way she looked made him seriously consider changing the office dress code.

"What are you doing here?" She leaned a shoulder against the open door and rubbed the top of one bare foot against the shapely calf of her other leg. Her toenails were painted red. "Is there a problem at the hotel? Did I forget something?"

No, but he'd forgotten just how sexy bare feet and red toenails on Geneva could be.

"Everything's fine."

"Is Teri's wedding still on?"

"As far as I know," he answered.

She looked puzzled. "Then I don't understand why you're here."

"I wanted to see you."

Not exactly the way he'd planned to phrase his response to the inevitable question, but true nonetheless. About that emptiness… It had started right after losing Geneva, although at the time he'd filled himself with anger. Then he'd moved through the who-needs-her stage and become a serial dater. But seeing her again, he'd discovered that when he was with her, the emptiness disappeared for a while. So here he was.

She frowned. "I don't get it."

"What part of 'I wanted to see you' is unclear?"

"If you're not here about work, that would make this a personal visit. On that subject, I don't think we have anything to say."

The way she looked, talking was the last thing on his mind. She always seemed to have that effect on him. "It's hot," he said. And he didn't just mean because his navy-blue shirt was absorbing the heat of the sun on his back. "Would you mind if I come in?"

"You're the boss."

Sometimes rank had its privileges and this was one of those times. He stepped inside, onto the tile entryway and looked around as she closed the door. To his right was a window seat and a plantation-shutter covered window above it. A stairway on the left led to the second floor and her bedroom. A year ago, she'd just moved in and hadn't picked out furniture. She'd borrowed money against this place to pay him back and he wondered if she'd been able to afford more than just the king-size bed now.

In the family room straight ahead, a light green corner group and matching recliner formed a conversation area around the media niche and fireplace. A bank of windows looked out over the Vegas Valley with a view of the Strip between here and the jagged jut of mountains in the distance. The adjacent kitchen with its abundance of white cupboards, onyx granite countertops and black refrigerator and microwave was a study in black and white.

"The place looks good."

"It's coming along," she said, glancing around.

But he saw the shadows flitting over her face and remembered what she'd said about conceiving their baby here. He'd expected irritation for luring her to Pinnacle that night, but he hadn't counted on the barrage of happy memories about the times they'd shared. And no way had he been prepared for the grief in Geneva's eyes when she'd mentioned the baby.

The tears she'd stubbornly held back had tugged at him and he'd had to see her. "About why I'm here—"

"I'm all ears," she said, folding her arms over her chest.

If only that were true, he thought, permitting

himself a quick glance at the intriguing things her knit top did to her breasts.

"I've been working hard," he began. "It's time for some fun."

"Good for you." She pumped her arm. "Seriously, Michael, you don't need my permission to let your hair down. You're a grown-up."

Who needed another grown-up to play with and he refused to let her put business between them.

"The thing is," he continued, "you've been working hard, too. And I could use some company on my quest for fun."

"You're asking me?"

"That was the general idea."

Her gaze narrowed. "What's going on, Michael?"

"You make it sound like I'm a CIA operative and this is a political plot."

"You got the plot part right. At least that's how it's beginning to feel. First an underhanded ruse and a clandestine dinner. *With* flowers and my favorite wine."

"I should be flogged."

"Now," she continued, a small smile betraying her, "you're skulking around here with an invitation for fun."

"Forget the flogging. Firing squad on Las Vegas Boulevard. We'll shut it down and sell tickets. That'll be fun."

"Stop," she said, laughing. "You're impossible."

"I've been taking lessons from you." He stared

down at her, so small. So feminine. So delicate. So irresistible. "So, what do you say? Are you up for some R & R?"

"No."

He tapped his ear as if he hadn't heard right. "Excuse me?"

Self-consciously she brushed strands of hair off her forehead. "I've been cleaning. I look like I've been through a natural disaster. If you'd bothered to call *before* you were already standing on my front porch, I could have saved you the trip."

This negative response was why he hadn't. The phone would have made it too easy for her.

"How can you be so cruel?"

She blinked. "Excuse me?"

"It's a hard-hearted woman who can turn down an invitation from a lonely bachelor."

"Oh, please. It's absolutely not possible that Las Vegas's most eligible bachelor is lonely."

You're wrong, Geneva, he thought. "And who's responsible for the fact that I'm a bachelor?"

Uncomfortable, she rubbed her nose. "And I've apologized more than once."

"I know. And I forgive you."

A suspicious expression replaced her discomfort. "Are you messing with my mind again?"

"No kidding around." He sighed. "I know you had your reasons."

"Really?"

He nodded. "When Teri and I had our talk about her second thoughts, I found myself quoting you."

"You did?"

"Almost word for word. Geneva Porter, my muse."

"Wow."

"Yeah." He shrugged. "I understand better now."

"I'm glad."

"Okay. About that fun—"

She held up her hand. "I can't, Michael."

"If it's about the way you look—" He didn't think she could look more beautiful. If he could bottle her appeal and sell it over the counter, he'd make millions.

"It's not that." She sighed. "We've finally put the past to rest. We're friends again."

Friends? He wasn't feeling friendly. He was feeling like he wanted to touch her, test the softness of her skin with his hands, taste her lips to see if they were as intoxicating as that night at the Garden of Love.

"And your point?" he asked, moving closer.

"I'm not a good risk. It wouldn't be smart to date."

"Don't be so sure."

Michael had her in his arms, his mouth on hers, before she could say no. In the blink of an eye or the beat of a heart, her initial surprise gave way to a sigh of surrender. So easily. Had she been yearning for this as much as he had? The thought drained most of the blood from his head and sent it south of his belt. Geneva linked her arms around his neck and settled herself against him. They were pressed together from chest to knee and there was no way she could miss how much he wanted her.

This was no sweet, "friendly" touching of mouths. It quickly escalated into moans, groans, heavy breathing and a mating of tongues. His heart was pounding in his chest as her breathy sounds of pleasure heated his blood and threatened to push him over the edge. Before he was completely gone, he pulled his mouth from hers. He'd only meant to show her that seeing each other again was a good idea.

Michael sucked in air and steadied himself before cupping her face in his palms and dropping a quick kiss on her full lips. Then he put a safe distance between him and that curvy body that could bring him to his knees.

Before he left, he'd give her something to think about. He grinned the grin she'd once told him would tempt a card-carrying commitment phobe.

"While you're dusting, there's something I want you to think about."

"W-what?" The pulse at the base of her throat was going wild.

"You just kissed me within a millimeter of your self-control, but you won't go out on a date with me. What's wrong with this picture?"

He whistled tunelessly as he opened the door and let himself out, hoping the breathless woman he'd just walked away from was just as frustrated as he was.

* * *

That kiss had nothing to do with why Geneva let Michael talk her into coming to this very public hospital event. No, he'd talked her into this by playing the publicity card, dangling the possibility of them as a couple in front of the press. But the kiss was never very far from her thoughts.

She glanced at him, so handsome in his black tux. Her heart skidded into slip and slide mode, reminding her how easily the touch of his lips and the feel of his body had made her forget all her resolutions to keep things between them strictly business. She looked around at the full tables in a banquet room at Caesar's Palace. She and Michael were now alone at a table for six while the other four people waited on stage to make speeches.

Michael was the guest of honor.

She met his gaze. "So tell me why Lily of the Valley Hospital is honoring you at this bash. Did you build the nuns a new bingo hall?"

"You're supposed to be nice to me," he reminded her. "People are watching. We don't want any frowning photos of you to show up in *People* magazine."

"Sorry." She sighed and tried again. "So what did you do?"

"Just a donation."

"Right." And he was *just* in construction.

She glanced around at the flowers, candles, chandeliers and linen tablecloths. If the designer duds and expensive jewels in this room were auctioned on eBay, they'd bring enough money to feed a third world country for quite a while. Dinners like this could cost a thousand dollars a plate and up, and one didn't get to be guest of honor by buying a couple boxes of cookies.

"Donations are tax deductible," she said.

One corner of his mouth curved up. "Don't tell me. You're undercover for the IRS."

"Go ahead and tease. But I know a donation that makes you the guest of honor has to be an investment in Sullivan Towers. I saw film crews from all the local stations here. Everyone has a vested interest in quality medical care. So choosing to give money to the hospital gives you a lot of bang for your marketing buck."

Before he could answer, the overhead lights dimmed and the speakers lined up beside the lectern. Geneva turned her chair to face the stage and Michael settled his beside her—so close she could feel his thigh through the thin black chiffon of her dress.

Then a spotlight landed on the man at the microphone who introduced himself as the regional vice president in charge of Lily of the Valley Hospital. After introducing everyone on stage, he thanked a lot of people for their hard work in putting together the dinner to honor local developer, Michael Sullivan. He directed the audience's attention to a large screen where pictures appeared.

Geneva saw one image after another of babies,

tiny scraps of humanity connected to machines by wires and tubes. A fist squeezed her heart and she swallowed hard to clear the emotion gathering in her throat. She was mesmerized by the before and after shots of the unbelievably small premature infants who survived and grew into healthy, gurgling babies thanks to the hospital's Neonatal Intensive Care Unit, open and operating because of Michael Sullivan's generosity.

Sensations flashed through her like a laser light show and she didn't know which one to address first. Actually that wasn't true. Pond scum was a start in describing how she felt about minimizing his gift to the hospital. Of all the causes in all the world, he'd helped the babies. One tear slid from the corner of her eye. She was lower than the sludge scraped off a sneaker.

The rest of the tribute passed in a haze and Geneva was numb. For the remainder of the evening, it was incredibly easy to smile adoringly at Michael, and she hoped all the right words came out of her mouth.

When they were back in the limo heading west on I-215 toward her house in Henderson, she could finally ask the question she'd been holding back.

"Why didn't you stop me, Michael?"

"I thought you wanted the cheesecake."

"No. When I was being a snarky witch, going on about bingo and getting bang for your buck. You didn't make that donation for the tax write-off or the media attention."

"I didn't?" There was amusement in his tone, but outside lights flashing over his features showed traces of emotion in his eyes.

"No. It was because of our baby girl, wasn't it?"

He was quiet for so long it seemed he wasn't going to answer. Finally he said, "Yes. It was for our baby."

A flash of remembered pain brought tears to her eyes, but she blinked them away. "The NICU is incredible. The pictures were amazing, especially the ones of the babies that fit into the palm of your hand."

"Without that NICU, those babies wouldn't make it," he said. "The equipment is high precision and intricate. It's extremely specialized. Even the beds are dedicated just to the infants. The tents are specially designed with heating coils to precisely control a premature infant's temperature."

She was surprised. "You didn't just write a check, did you? You've done your homework."

He shrugged. "For the infants born too early, those machines make the difference between life and—" He stopped, his eyes dark in the shadows of the car. "Let's just say they survive and thrive. All those bells and whistles don't come cheap, but the hefty price tag buys technological miracles."

She sniffled. "I wish you could have bought a miracle for our baby."

"Me, too—" His voice cracked.

Geneva blinked and stared at him. She'd never seen Michael Sullivan crack. Not once, not ever. She could hardly believe it. Now she didn't just feel badly about teasing him tonight. It was worse than that.

"We never talked about her, Michael. One minute I had a life growing inside me. The next she was gone."

"I know."

The limo pulled to a stop under the streetlight in front of her house. With the car's privacy window up, they could continue the conversation without the driver overhearing.

"It was the hardest thing I've ever gone through." Including her childhood. "I was only three months along. I never had the chance to feel her move. She never got big enough for me to feel her little feet or elbows. I didn't get big and fat and uncomfortable—all the things pregnant women feel before giving birth. I'd give anything to know what it feels like to waddle—"

"Geneva—" When she sniffled again, Michael took her hand and laced his fingers with hers. "I don't know what to say."

"It's okay." She tried to smile, but her mouth quivered. "It helps to talk about it. We never did."

"That was a rough time—"

"It's a blur. Wedding plans moved forward at warp speed," she remembered. "I guess the hardest thing for me was that we didn't grieve—"

"We were together," he protested. "That night I took you to the E.R."

She recalled doubling over with cramps and the horror at seeing the blood. Michael had gathered her in his arms and rushed her to the hospital, but it was too late. Michael held her and stayed until she slept.

"Yes, you were there. Thank God. I'd never have gotten through it without you." She looked at him and squeezed the hand she held. "But after that night we never talked about what happened, Michael. No one else loved that baby girl like we did." Her voice caught and the tears in her eyes made his features blur. "I wanted our child so much."

"I wanted her, too." Michael pulled her onto his lap and folded her in his arms. "Not a day goes by that I don't think about her, Geneva. She'd be a year old now."

"Probably walking," she said.

"And talking. Starting to, anyway."

Geneva felt his chest rise and fall as he took a shuddering breath. She rested her cheek on his shoulder and slid her arms around his neck as she snuggled close. When his arms tightened in response, she knew there was no need for him to say more. Words couldn't convey what they felt—the profound grief and loss. Sharing the burden with Michael somehow made it lighter.

It was ironic, she thought. She'd accompanied him tonight because she felt she owed him and if it would help him get the financing for Sullivan Towers, she could pretend to be a couple. But she realized now that they would always be connected because they'd made a child together and mourned her.

The reality of that would bind them forever.

His breath stirred her hair when he whispered in her ear, "The doctor said we could try again. When you felt better." He nuzzled her neck. "You feel pretty good to me."

Geneva smiled through her grief. "Thanks for the offer. But I think it's best I go inside."

"How about a rain check?" he asked hopefully.

"It wouldn't be very smart."

But when she was inside and heard the car pull away, she didn't want to be smart. She wanted to be with Michael.

CHAPTER NINE

A FEW days ago Geneva had been in this limo with Michael when he'd made his indecent proposal. Those few days should have been enough time to restore rational thought. But the only thoughts she'd had were warm and fuzzy and filled with the man who missed their baby as much as she did. She'd assumed he'd simply moved on without looking back, but she'd been wrong. What else was she wrong about? And how was she supposed to resist him?

The answer was simple. She couldn't.

Which explained why after weeks of turning down his invitations, she'd finally accepted earlier today when he'd asked her to dinner. He'd sent the limo for her. Probably something had come up at the office and he would meet her at the restaurant.

Smoothing the silk over her knees, she fretted that this simple, sleeveless black dress wasn't fancy enough. But Michael hadn't said where they were going.

She didn't care. Her stomach was tied in so many knots, there was no room for food. The nerves, she realized, were anticipation. That was stupid in so many ways, she didn't know where to start. But lately, as far as Michael was concerned, she'd learned that prudence and rational thought were highly overrated.

Not to mention lonely.

The car turned left, then stopped at a guard gate. She'd been so wrapped up in thoughts of Michael, she hadn't noticed they were driving away from the Las Vegas Strip and into a residential area.

Geneva pushed a button and lowered the window between her and the driver. "Excuse me. But where are we going?"

"I have orders from Mr. Sullivan to drive you to his home."

"Oh." Because he needed to change for dinner, Geneva hoped.

The car slowed at a second set of gates and the driver punched numbers into a keypad.

"Open sesame," she said.

"What's that, Miss Porter?" The good-looking man in his early fifties glanced at her in the rearview mirror.

"I said this is a beautiful area."

"Yes, ma'am."

Grass, trees and shrubs, all perfectly manicured, lined the road where houses—make that mansions— sat on huge lots. They passed a manmade lake and finally pulled into a circular driveway at the end of a cul-de-sac. She slid over and glanced out the window at the imposing white stucco structure with a red tile roof. A turret in front gave it the look of a castle and, although it was dusk, spotlights picked out flowers and bushes.

Then the driver opened her door, and said, "Mr. Sullivan is expecting you."

She nodded and walked up the steps to the double door entry. Before she could knock, it opened and Michael was there, as if he'd been watching and waiting for her.

"Hi."

"Geneva." He smiled. "Come in."

He stepped aside and she walked into the grand, two-story entry, trying to take it all in—tall ceilings, curved staircase with birch-topped wrought-iron rail, tile, thick beige carpet. The living room was spacious and elegant with its sofas and cherry wood tables.

"Michael, this is beautiful." She turned, and that's when she noticed he wasn't dressed for dinner. Correction, not for a fancy restaurant dinner.

He'd been completely amazing in his tux the other night, but the worn jeans and white cotton shirt with long sleeves rolled up was a look that reached another level of amazing. He was barefoot, and pretty much defined the word sexy. Gone for the moment was the powerful CEO of Sullivan, Inc. In his place was the man who'd grieved with her for their baby.

This was the man who could break her heart.

With an effort, she dragged her gaze from his feet to his face. "I thought you said we were going out to dinner."

"I believe I asked you to have dinner with me."

She thought for a moment, then abandoned the effort. She'd been had and couldn't find the will to care. "I'm overdressed."

He turned away, giving her a spectacular view of his wide shoulders and world-class butt. "It's not a problem. Don't worry about it."

Don't worry? How could she not? The last time she'd been in this situation, she'd ended up in bed with him. Her heart pounded so hard, so fast, it was just this side of pain. "Don't worry" joined "I'll be in touch" as the most unsettling words in the English language.

And what did it mean? That he didn't care that she was overdressed? Or that it didn't matter because he planned to take the dress off her?

In the kitchen, a cavernous room with silver appliances and miles of cupboards topped by granite counters, she noticed two crystal flutes and a bottle of champagne.

"Are we celebrating?" she asked.

He grinned. "You finally said yes to me. I think that's cause for celebration."

Okay. She would decide how she felt about that later. "This is a beautiful house."

"Maybe you should reserve judgment. You haven't had a tour of the upstairs yet. The master bedroom is why I bought the place."

Geneva was doing her best to resist him, but he was—deliberately, she suspected—making it tough. The mischievous gleam of invitation in his black eyes, the seductive tone in his whiskey on gravel voice, the veiled temptation to go to his bed were all weapons in an arsenal designed to sweep her off her feet. He so didn't need champagne. Being the focus of attention from this handsome, charismatic, charming man was ten times more intoxicating.

She took a bracing sip of the bubbly liquid anyway, then leaned against the island in the center of his kitchen. "I'm sure the second floor is just as intriguing as the first." Something flickered in his eyes and gave her a sense of power. "I can't quote your exact words, but you did say something about dinner."

"And I'm a man of my word." He held out a hand, indicating the backyard. "I'll see you to your table."

He took her hand and led her outside, which was no less impressive than the inside. The house overlooked the golf course. To the right, a pool and spa were tucked into a corner of the yard. A glass-topped iron table with flowers in the center was set for two. Steaks, salad, baked potatoes and biscuits were all ready and waiting.

It was simple. It was seductive. It was working.

And Mother Nature was his coconspirator in sin.

The underside of the sky's wispy clouds were painted pink and purple and gold by the setting sun. When it completely disappeared, there would be a big, full moon. The smell of the warm breeze off the desert mingled with the fresh scent of flowers and created a fragrance that promised mystery, magic and more. Romance. He'd turned it on full blast, and God help her, she was soaking it up like a dry sponge.

"How did you know I'd get here before the food got cold?"

"I'm not a man who leaves things to chance. Shall we?" he said.

Take a chance? She simply took a deep breath and jumped in. "Yes."

Michael held her chair, then sat at a right angle to her. He lifted his glass and said, "To possibilities."

She touched her flute to his, then sipped. The nerves were still twisting her stomach, but she found she really was hungry. And the food was good. She could add grilling steak to his list of talents.

"This is delicious," she said.

"I'm glad."

She met his gaze. "I didn't know you'd bought a house."

"I'm doing business here. What did you think I'd do?"

She wanted to think he'd bought the house and put down roots because she was there. How dumb was that?

"I figured you'd commute back and forth from New York. After everything that happened, I guess I didn't expect you to relocate."

He set down his fork and wiped his mouth on a linen napkin. "Real estate is always a good investment. And, I like it here—the area, the excitement, the people—"

The smolder and sparks in his eyes set fire to the feelings inside her. She crumbled the biscuit in her hands and let the pieces fall on her plate. "I like it, too."

He finished the last of his champagne. "They say it's the most exciting city on the planet."

And getting more exciting by the second. "Yeah, that's what they say."

She felt as if she needed air, but they were already outside. It wouldn't matter how wide-open her space, being near Michael was like playing with fire. And fire sucked all the oxygen from her lungs.

She stood, picked up her plate and carried it inside. Michael was right behind her when she set it in the sink. She shivered when he put his hands on her upper arms and turned her toward him.

"Geneva." Her name on his lips sounded exotic and beautiful. And so much like a caress. "You must know how I feel."

"No, I—" She shook her head but didn't miss her own need reflected in his black eyes.

"I want you."

"Why? How can you?" She searched his gaze. "I

rejected you. Making a commitment freaks me out. You should be thanking your lucky stars that you didn't get stuck with me."

"Once burned, twice shy?" he asked, the corners of his mouth curving up.

"Exactly."

"What if I said I did learn? I still want you—this time no strings attached."

Easy for him to say, she thought. The more she knew about Michael, the more those strings tightened and pulled her in.

"Isn't it just asking for trouble?"

Michael tightened his hold on her upper arms and drew her close as he stared into her eyes. Intensity darkened his own and her heart tilted. He touched his mouth to hers. The kiss was surprisingly sweet and gentle considering the tension she felt in him. Then he nibbled kisses over her chin and cheek, down her neck and concentrated a great deal of attention on the hollow just beneath her ear. She sucked in air and barely suppressed a moan of pleasure.

He touched his tongue to the ohmigod spot, then blew lightly, raising tingles on her skin. "Does that feel like trouble?"

"That was so not fair," she whispered.

"I want you," he repeated.

Then he grinned the grin that always took the starch out of her. When he easily swung her into his arms, he met her gaze and there was a question in his.

She knew he was telling her to speak now or forever hold her peace.

She held it and slid her arms around his neck as he carried her up the stairs for an intimate tour of the master bedroom.

The next morning Geneva rushed into her office and found her assistant and Teri Sullivan waiting for her.

"You're late," Chloe said, as she set a cup of coffee on the desk.

"I know. I'm sorry."

"Sorry doesn't cut it. You're never late," her assistant said, hands on hips.

"We have a meeting," Teri reminded her. "A status session on the wedding details."

Geneva set her briefcase and purse beside her chair and tried to catch her breath. Late was what happened when Michael Sullivan made love to you all night long.

She sat down and looked at Teri. "Okay. I wanted to talk to you about the menu. Finger foods and hors d'oeuvres. Innovation is the new elegant. So, let's get started."

"Not so fast, boss. Are you okay?" Chloe looked concerned.

"I'm fine. Now if you could pull the Sullivan/ Smith wedding file."

"I was worried," Chloe continued. "You didn't call. I couldn't get you on your cell."

Geneva pulled it from her purse and checked the bars. "No charge."

She'd been at Michael's and the charger was at home. Being wrapped in Michael's arms hadn't left much room for coherent thought, let alone details like phone charging.

She looked at Chloe. "As you said, I'm never late. Therefore, I'm unfamiliar with tardiness protocol. Next time, I'll call."

Her assistant's blue eyes narrowed. "You're already planning a next time?"

"You bet," Geneva shot back. "Right after I go over the wall and take the other prisoners with me."

"Excuse me for being concerned."

"I appreciate it," Geneva said. She'd find a way to smooth Chloe's feelings after her meeting. "But I don't want to keep Teri waiting any longer. The file?"

"It's on your desk," Chloe said, then walked to the door and closed it.

"You're looking fabulous," she said to Teri.

"Thanks. So are you." Teri sat in one of the chairs in front of the desk then fixed Geneva with a probing stare. "In fact, you're positively glowing."

"Too much sun."

Too much Michael probably. On second thought, she decided, there was no such thing. Last night had been…perfect.

"There's a sparkle in your eyes, Geneva. What's that about? And don't tell me sun." She crossed one long leg over the other, settling in. "Obviously Chloe is concerned because you're never late. What's up?"

"What's up is that I've apparently become a creature of habit. Predictable." She stood and started pacing. "Clearly I need to vary my routine so that when I'm a few minutes late—"

"Try an hour."

"That much?" She stopped and stared at the other woman. "I didn't think it would take that long to go home and change."

"Go home?" Teri sat up straight. "Change? Now we're getting somewhere. I'll take a wild guess that there's a man involved. My brother is late, too—" Her eyes grew wide. "You and my brother?"

Geneva sat and rested her elbows on her desk as she cupped her face in her hands. "Don't make me tell you."

"Oh, please." Teri just looked at her.

Hesitating a moment, Geneva finally said, "It's important to me that you understand something. I didn't refuse to marry Michael because I didn't care. Just the opposite."

"Look, Geneva, while neither one of us was looking, we've kind of slipped back into that friendship thing we had going on."

"Yeah. I've noticed. And I like it. Which is why I need to keep this to myself."

She did care about Teri. But Teri was Michael's sister and the only family he had. Last night had proven it was pointless for Geneva to pretend she and Michael were only about business. She hadn't figured out what to do about that, except she knew that what happened at his house should stay at his house. And it shouldn't happen again.

Teri tucked a strand of dark hair behind her ear. "I guess we need to clear the air. Any hard feelings I had for you are gone. They disappeared right about the time I had a meltdown about my wedding. When Michael told me about your background all the resentment went away."

"I guess it runs in the family."

"So admit it. You and Michael did the wild thing. He's the man who made you late."

"He made me a lot of things. Late is just one of them." She shook her head. "I shouldn't be telling you this."

"Why not?"

"It's the night of the rehearsal dinner all over again." Geneva needed to talk now as much as she had then, but it wasn't fair to dump on his sister.

"What if I swear that I won't be an insensitive water buffalo? The thing is, I care about you. And I love my brother. He's been different lately. Like he's more alive since—"

"When?"

Teri's gaze was direct. "Since you."

"Don't say that." Geneva covered her face with her hands. "I'm wrong for him. I have no clue what a fulfilling relationship looks like. Michael and I—It can't happen again."

"Really? Why?"

Geneva dropped her hands. "Because Michael doesn't love me."

"He asked you to marry him."

"That was because I was pregnant with his child. The night before the wedding I asked him if he loved me and he said 'of course.' I'm the first to admit that reassurance was important to me. I hate to say needy, but—" She shrugged. "Marriage is too big a step to take without love to back it up. Then you told me not to worry because Michael always does the right thing. I got the message. He was going through with the wedding because he's an honorable man."

"Honorable men have feelings, too."

"I never said he didn't." Geneva sighed. "But basing a marriage on doing the right thing is so *not* doing the right thing."

"Michael doesn't talk about feelings," Teri said. "He's a man—"

"That's not breaking news."

Geneva had seen him naked. Again. And it was even better this time around. He'd said no strings attached. But saying it and getting the message through to her heart were two different things. This time, if she wasn't careful, the fall when it came would be even worse.

Teri shook her head. "I didn't mean that. Women talk about this stuff. Men don't. And Michael clams up even more than most. He's afraid to say I love you."

"He's not afraid of anything," Geneva said.

"You're not the only one dealing with a past. Did Michael ever tell you about the last time he saw our parents?"

"No." Geneva caught her breath.

"I was young, but I'll never forget. I guess trauma highlights that stuff." Teri's eyes filled with the shadows of remembering.

"What happened?"

"Mom teased Michael about being too cool to tell her he loved her. It was just a mom thing. Like make sure you have on clean underwear in case you have an accident and wind up in the E.R. She said it might be the last time he had a chance to say he loved her. He acted like a typical teenage jerk and didn't. But her warning was prophetic." Teri leaned forward. "I'm no shrink, but my theory is that in Michael's mind, those three words mean goodbye. And he never says it to me."

"But you know he loves you."

"I do. The thing is, he's a show-don't-tell kind of guy. In every way possible, he lets me know how he feels. He just doesn't say the words."

"Some of us need the words. Especially when he disappears into work."

Teri sighed. "That started after losing our parents, too. He poured his grief into action and turned it into success."

Like pouring a lot of money into the hospital for a Neonatal Intensive Care Unit. The passion and energy he was putting into Sullivan Towers.

Geneva knew misery was brimming in her eyes. "Teri, I don't want to hurt him again."

"So you'll back off without giving it a try?"

"Yes. It would be better for him."

Teri stood. "Would you rather have a guy who says I love you all the time but is shallow as a cookie sheet? Or one who shows he cares in everything he does?"

"That's a no brainer. But—"

Teri held up a hand. "Something else…he'd kill me for telling you this." She thought a moment. "He'd kill me for this whole conversation. But here it is. I understand you walked out because you care about my brother. You need to know he didn't ask you to marry him because of the baby."

"You don't know that."

"Yeah, I do. He could have been a father without marrying you. It happens all the time. Michael Sullivan has dated a lot of women and never proposed to any of them. You're the only woman he ever asked to marry him."

"I didn't know," Geneva said.

"He'd take a risk in business without batting an eye. But until you, I never saw him take a chance with his heart." Teri slung her purse over her shoulder. "I have to go. We can reschedule our meeting."

Absently Geneva nodded. Her head was spinning. She wasn't the only one who hadn't shared her darker side. Michael had held back, too. Stoic, solid, supportive Michael Sullivan. He was there for everyone, but who was there for him?

She wanted to be, she realized. She'd wanted to share everything before. But she'd been so sure Michael was going to marry her simply to keep his word. Had she been wrong? Was she so screwed up that she didn't recognize love when it was staring her in the face?

Right now she was numb and she wanted to stay that way. Because Michael was only looking for no-strings-attached. She'd had her chance and thrown it away. When the pain hit, it would be bad. And she had no one to blame but herself.

CHAPTER TEN

GENEVA studied the empty lot adjoining the Sullivan Hotel. The ribbon-cutting ceremony and ground-breaking festivities were fast approaching. After Teri left, Geneva had kept her scheduled appointment with Michael to hammer out final details for this event. It gave her a good excuse to put off thinking about the horrible mistake she'd made. Even though their meeting required hiking around in the dirt in her high heels, it was hard to hold off the pain when Michael was standing right there.

With hands on hips and sunglasses shielding his eyes, he surveyed the land. "This is a good spot for the ribbon cutting."

"Okay." She made a note on a diagram. "Then I think we should set up the media over there. Cutting the ribbon is a photo op, so let's make the most of it. When they start snapping pictures, the Strip will be in the background."

"Good idea," he said, nodding.

It was getting close to lunchtime and already hot, but she knew the mercury would continue climbing until at least five o'clock. Since the Sullivan Towers weekend blowout would be in September, hot weather was a given. "I think we should set up a canopy," she said, tapping her pen on her lip.

"Now?"

"That would be lovely," she said, smiling.

"I'll see what I can do." The corners of his mouth lifted and probably there was a gleam in his eyes behind those dark lenses.

"And if I snapped my fingers and wiggled my nose, would you point me to the pot of gold at the end of the rainbow?"

He tipped the glasses down and met her gaze. "You're being a smart aleck."

"I am. You may remember that from time to time the wacky side of my personality surfaces." Bantering with him like this was one of her favorite things. She would miss it. No strings attached meant nothing to tie them together and that meant they'd be over.

"Let's see." He folded his arms over his chest. "I remember that you like your eggs over medium so you can dip toast in the yolk. You're probably the only woman on the planet who doesn't take her chocolate straight up—nuts, caramel, or toffee must be involved. A movie requires at least twenty minutes lead time to avoid crashing around in the dark with the obligatory popcorn and diet drink. And for everything else you're also the only woman I've ever known who's persistently and painfully punctual."

She stared at him and struggled not to let her bottom jaw drop. He'd nailed her. "Wow."

Memories of him, her, naked and tangled in sheets flashed through her mind.

He looked at her. "Define 'wow.'"

"Wow means I can't believe you remembered all that."

"I'm good with details."

He certainly was; she could testify to it. But there were details, and there were *details*. Business was one thing. Personal was something else entirely, and he'd gotten very personal. Geneva wondered if it was true that she was important to him. Maybe once. Now she didn't know what to believe and suddenly she couldn't stop the question.

"Why did you go through with the deal to buy the hotel, Michael?"

"It made good business sense."

That wasn't what she wanted to hear. "Was that the only reason?"

"What other reason is there? I'm a businessman. Real estate development is the cornerstone of my corporation. This property was losing money and it shouldn't have been."

"So you saw an opportunity and grabbed it?"

"Of course."

She winced. Those two words resurrected a whole lot of emotional baggage for her. "I see."

"This property should be successful. It's a great location and there's room for development."

"Okay. Let me rephrase," she said. "Why did you go through with the deal after we broke up?"

He'd already told her it was because he was over her, but just hours ago she'd come from his bed. How over her was he?

"You're asking if my reasons had anything to do with you?"

That's what she was asking and if he said "of course," she would stomp his sunglasses into the dirt. If he said "no way," at least she'd know where she stood. Then she would let in the pain, as if she could stop it anyway. She'd go through all the stages of grief and move on. Probably. Maybe.

"Yes."

He slid his sunglasses to the top of his head. His gaze met hers. "I thought about backing out. But—"

"But what?"

"I wanted to do this project. For my parents. Something I built. Something tangible. For them."

Emotion tightened in her chest. She took a deep breath before saying, "I'm sure they'd be so proud of you."

"That's not the only reason I went forward."

"What else?"

"You were here," he said.

What did that mean? Her heart stopped for two beats and when rhythm resumed, there was nothing normal about it.

Did she dare ask? "And buying the house? Putting down roots here?"

"Same reason."

What about no strings attached? She wasn't brazen enough to ask the question. But there was something she wanted him to know.

"I had a talk with Teri earlier," she said.

He frowned. "About the wedding?"

"It was supposed to be."

"Uh-oh. I'm afraid to ask."

"We got into some personal issues," she admitted.

"About you and me?"

You. Me. Last night. She sighed. "About that punctuality thing of mine? You aren't the only one who noticed. Teri was waiting for me and she guessed—about us."

"Swell," he said, in a tone that meant it was anything but.

"I didn't want to talk about it."

"But she twisted your arm." He wasn't asking.

"Kind of. She told me about what happened with your mother before that last trip with your dad."

His mouth pulled tight. "I'm going to kill her."

"She said you'd say that. And—" She studied him. "You don't look surprised."

"Because I'm not. Teri's been analyzing me since she took Psych 101 in college."

"Is she right?"

"She couldn't be more wrong."

"Okay." She caught her bottom lip between her teeth. "But I had a thought."

"There's a dangerous prospect."

He was trying to distract her and it wouldn't work. "I read somewhere that sorrows are our best educators. That we can see further through a tear than a telescope."

He frowned. "And you think this is a profound statement."

"Yes. Sorrow is difficult under any circumstances. But combined with guilt—it's an incredibly heavy burden. I didn't get a chance to hold our baby and actually be a mom. But I was pregnant long enough to think about the awesome, incredible responsibility of molding a human being."

"And your point?" His tone was clipped.

"I think your mother would be devastated if she, however inadvertently, said or did anything to negatively impact your life. She was teasing. If she'd come home, you'd never have thought twice about that goodbye."

"I appreciate the thought." He curved his fingers around her upper arm. "Now I've got one."

"Care to share? Or do I have to channel someone to find out?"

"I think it's time to get you in out of the sun. It's hot and we should go to lunch."

"That's actually three separate thoughts." She badly wanted to ask him another question, but held back. "And, like I said earlier, we need to put up a canopy for the ribbon-cutting ceremony."

"I agree. People passing out from heat stroke isn't the kind of publicity we're after."

He'd said that once before, when he'd told her why he didn't release her from her contract. She almost wished he had let her go. It would have been easier than getting to know him. Finding out he was a special man. Finding out she'd had a chance to get everything she'd ever wanted and had blown it.

When pain squeezed her heart, she pulled out her sense of humor. It was the only defense she had left.

"You did say you wanted a three-ring circus. We could erect a tent, get tigers, elephants and a guy who walks on stilts."

As they moved into the shade at the hotel entrance, his gaze narrowed on her. "Remind me later to have a serious talk about this wacky side of your personality."

"Yeah. You might be sorry about putting down those roots."

She was sorry because he was so near and had never been further out of her reach.

Michael breathed a sigh of relief when he finished his last media interview Saturday night. So far, the grand opening weekend of Sullivan Towers had far exceeded his expectations. The ribbon-cutting ceremony the day before had gone off without a hitch and the sales office was immediately swamped with serious buyers. Monday he'd talk numbers with Dex, but everything was looking even better than he'd hoped.

From the beginning he'd known the project was a moneymaker, but getting the brand name in front of the public had been the key. Geneva had been an important component, however reluctant she'd been initially. In the beginning he'd been using her, and she'd agreed because she owed him. But working together had developed into much more than business.

He and Geneva had started this gala doing joint interviews, but she'd been called away. All of a sudden it became very important that he share tonight's success with his extraordinary events planner.

And what an event she'd planned. She had arranged four large screens in the corners of the room that constantly flashed alternating scenes of an artist's conception of the Towers' grounds, an architect's rendering of the building and a virtual tour of the floor plans. Tables and chairs were grouped around the screens for leisurely dining after guests filled their plates at the four gourmet buffet stations. Melina St. George had created a signature Sullivan dish that would be featured at Pinnacle. Waiters in black pants and short white jackets circulated with trays of champagne. In the center of the room, a tuxedo-clad musician caressed the ivory keys of a grand piano.

The opening was everything he'd told her he wanted—and she'd pulled it off as promised—a smooth combination of comfort, class and sophistication.

Impatience rippled through him as he looked around. Finding Geneva shouldn't be this hard. After all, she was wearing that eye-popping dress. He didn't quite buy what she'd said about orange being the new black and he didn't care. Not a single woman in any color of the rainbow could wear a dress like Geneva.

Finally the crowd parted slightly, and Michael caught a glimpse of vibrant color. There she was, dressed in flowing orange silk that clung to every feminine curve but left one slender shoulder bare. She was incredibly sexy, impossibly beautiful. An irresistible beacon.

An irresistible beacon talking and laughing with a man Michael thought looked vaguely familiar. Some actor. The knot in his gut pulled tighter as he noticed other men watching her, too. He recognized the yearning expression in their eyes because he was flooded with the feeling every time he was with her.

But what he really hated was the way the weasel she was with didn't miss an opportunity to touch her. In the short time it took him to weave his way through the crush of bodies and get to her, the guy had managed to kiss her hand. Irrational jealousy surged through him when she laughed at something the guy said.

He stopped beside her. "Geneva."

"Michael." She smiled with genuine pleasure. "Did you finish with the reporters?"

"Yes. Are you going to introduce me?" he asked, taking the other man's measure.

"Of course. Michael Sullivan, this is Connor Flynn. We met at CineVegas when his latest movie premiered here."

The two men shook hands and Michael frowned, struggling to control his inner idiot. "Welcome to Sullivan Towers."

"Thank you. I've put a deposit on one of the penthouse units." Connor's voice had traces of an Irish accent. Women would find that appealing, which Michael found annoying as hell. "It's a great place you've got here."

"My team has worked above and beyond the call of duty. I'm glad you like the results." Michael wondered how he could sound so civilized when he felt anything but. It was business, he reminded himself. Except it felt very personal as he stared at Geneva. "I've been looking for you."

"Is everything all right?"

It wouldn't be if this guy touched her again, Michael thought. "I just wanted you to know the votes are in and the verdict is unanimous. You throw a great party."

"That's the truth," Connor agreed. "Darling, say the word and you could have a career in Hollywood. There's always an event going on. You'd have more work than you could handle."

Michael swore silently when the creep draped his arm over her shoulder and brushed one finger up and down her bare skin. He knew if he didn't get Geneva to himself in the next thirty seconds, this event wouldn't be about his residential high-rise. It would be about the rise this two-bit Don Juan got out of him.

"She has a contract with this hotel. And I need her," he said, taking her hand and slipping it into the bend of his arm. He kept his fingers on hers, holding her to him. "Enjoy yourself, Connor."

But not with this woman.

"See you later," she said over her shoulder.

Not if Michael could help it.

"Do you really need me for something?"

"No." At least not for work.

Geneva blew out a long breath as she held on to him with both hands. "Then you're my knight in shining armor."

"Oh?"

"And it's about time you rescued me." She glanced over her shoulder and shuddered. "I swear, if he'd touched me one more time…" She met his gaze. "Suffice it to say there would have been a scene and the resulting publicity wouldn't be the good kind."

Michael grinned. "It's a good thing I happened along

when I did then. Let me take a giant leap and guess you won't be visiting his penthouse in Sullivan Towers."

"Heaven forbid." She shuddered again. "I know you have a lot riding on sales, but it wouldn't break my heart if that one fell through."

That went double for him. "I don't think Connor Flynn will affect the success of this project."

"Me, either." Her eyes were shining as she looked around. "Look at this crowd, Michael. It's like R&F central."

"R&F?"

"Rich and famous," she explained. "If this isn't an unqualified success, I don't know what is. I've lost track of the number of people who told me they've reserved units."

"Things are looking very good," he admitted, staring at her mouth.

Her hair was pulled straight back from her face, a dramatic look that could have been severe if she didn't possess an innate sweetness. The style highlighted her eyes and mouth and when she smiled the sheer beauty of it went straight through him.

"Congratulations, Michael." She threw herself into his arms for a spontaneous hug. "I'm so happy for you."

With all her delicate curves up close and personal, he was pretty happy for himself. He folded her in his arms and breathed in the sweet scent of her. "I wouldn't be here without you."

He meant that, and not just about this event. The sudden and unexpected realization hit him hard and deep.

She stepped back. "We should find Teri and Dex. Compare notes—"

"I saw them," he said. "They were surrounded by reporters."

"How was that going?"

"Teri was flashing her engagement ring and appeared to be enjoying herself. Dex—"

"Is he holding up all right?"

"Yeah."

She frowned. "How can you be so sure?"

"Because Teri's by his side." He remembered that night at The Garden of Love when Geneva had said love was all that mattered. At the time he'd thought it ironic, coming from her. But overexposure to Geneva had changed his mind about a lot of things—especially about getting her out of his system.

"Media blitz two is already underway then," Geneva said. "The press will be salivating over a Sullivan bridal shower, the bachelor party, the—"

He touched a finger to her lips. "Let's just enjoy one triumph at a time."

"Okay."

He very much wanted to enjoy a few moments alone with Geneva.

"Come with me." He pulled her out a side door into the warm September night right after snagging two flutes of champagne from the tray of a passing waiter. Even in the subdued light outside he could see that her eyes glittered with excitement and the exhilaration of a job well done.

Michael handed her champagne, then touched his glass to hers. "Here's to a plan coming together."

"Amen," she said.

He had another plan that had nothing to do with business and everything to do with pleasure. He wanted to kiss her. He wanted to hear her breath catch followed by the small moan of pleasure that would drive him crazy.

The pulse at the base of her throat fluttered wildly. She grew very still and the way her gaze lingered on his mouth it was clear her thoughts matched his.

"So, you're happy with the way things are going?" Her voice was low, breathy, sexy.

"Very. You did a great job."

"I had lots of help," she said modestly. When she shrugged that bare shoulder, his pulse shot off the chart. Her smile was like seeing the sun come out after a long rain. "Still, I hope in some small way, I've made up for the past."

He held up his champagne flute. "Here's to my having the good sense not to fire you."

She touched her glass to his again. "I'm glad you're pleased."

"I am, yes. It's everything I asked for." But not everything he wanted.

He lowered his mouth to hers, tasting champagne and a momentary tremble of her lips that told him she wanted him, too. When he met her gaze again, he saw desire shining in her eyes, the feelings swirling inside her. He wanted her. He wanted a commitment. He wanted everything—her body, her heart, her soul.

But this wasn't the time to settle things between them the way they should be settled. It was true that you didn't appreciate what you had until it was gone. And he'd gone without her for a year.

By some miracle, he had another chance. As soon as everything calmed down, he would reconcile things with Miss Geneva Porter. He'd told her what he wanted for this grand opening event, but he hadn't told her how much he'd grown to want and need *her*.

Last time they'd gone too fast and everything had gone wrong. This time he would wait and do everything right.

CHAPTER ELEVEN

GENEVA leaned back in her desk chair and rubbed her tired eyes. As much as she hated computers, the Internet was a useful tool for gathering information, whether it was flowers, food or just a concept for an event. The question she'd been asked repeatedly to the point of irritation was where she got her ideas. The night of the Towers grand opening a week ago, she'd been tempted to tell the reporter that her ideas came from the idea store. But she'd held back.

Shortly after, Michael had ended the interview and they'd gotten separated. She hadn't seen him again until he'd rescued her from that incredibly egotistical, arrogant actor who had behaved as if he were God's gift to the female population. If his wandering hands had "accidentally" grazed her breast or backside one more time, she'd have given him the slap heard around the world.

But Michael made it all better when he'd taken her

outside for champagne and a kiss that had gone to her head way before the alcohol. She would always remember the night because it had been a professional triumph and she'd thought a personal one as well. She'd sworn the look in his eyes had held a promise. But she hadn't seen him alone since that night. She was beginning to wonder if she'd been wrong. God knows it wouldn't be the first time where Michael was concerned.

"Hey, boss." Chloe walked into her office. "These messages came in while I was holding your calls."

Geneva took the slips of paper and quickly glanced through to see if any were from Michael. Nada. Sighing, she searched her desk for a clear space to set the messages so they wouldn't disappear in the clutter before she had a chance to read them. There was a tiny spot on the outer edge and she set them down.

Chloe settled them more securely on the corner. "Is there anything else you need before I leave?"

She needed Michael shaken until his perfect, pearly-white teeth rattled. Or maybe she was the one who needed a good swift kick in the keister. A wake-up call. A reality check. She had an imagination and knew how to use it because apparently she'd imagined the moment between her and Michael that night was a *moment* with a capital M. And if she could keep up this level of indignation, maybe she could hold off the hurt.

"Earth to boss?"

She blinked and realized Chloe was waiting for an answer. "Oh. There's nothing else. Go home."

"Right back at you."

"Soon." Geneva tucked her hair behind her ears. "Teri Sullivan's coming by after work to discuss her wedding."

"You've put in a lot of man hours on that. I guess I should say woman hours. And I know a beautiful, perfect wedding is every little girl's dream, yada yada. But—" she put her right hand in the air "—I swear if I ever get married, it's going to be I-do-I-do-too at the justice of the peace."

"I'm kind of partial to The Garden of Love. A hundred and fifty dollars. That includes rings and a limo."

And a kiss guaranteed to sweep a girl off her feet in spite of all the reasons she should have stood firm and resisted.

"I'll keep it in mind." Chloe wiggled her fingers in a goodbye.

"Night, Chlo."

Teri would be there any minute and Geneva needed to be up to speed. She grabbed the Sullivan/Smith file and glanced through it. The time-sensitive details had been taken care of but flowers and food needed to be locked in soon.

"Hello." A light knock drew her attention to the doorway.

"Hi, Teri." Geneva forced a carefree smile, then

glanced at her desk. "Have a seat. Sorry everything is such a mess. I've been busy."

"That would explain it."

"What?" Geneva met her gaze.

"Why you look tired."

"Well, you look radiant." Geneva was determined to get through this meeting without dumping on Michael's sister. "How's Dex?"

"Good. Up to his fine-looking rear in alligators."

"Oh?"

"He's locking down the details for the project financing. He and Michael have been joined at the hip for days."

"So you haven't seen much of him?"

"Not as much as I'd like, but we have dinner together every night. Although sometimes it's more of a bedtime snack."

So much for the he-was-too-busy-to-see-her theory. Dex managed to find time with his fiancée. But his intended hadn't left him at the altar. Because they hadn't been to the altar yet, and if Geneva didn't get her head back in the game, that altar would be naked.

"How do you feel about flowers?"

"I'm all in favor," Teri answered.

"Do you have any preferences?"

Teri tapped her lip. "I love roses. And there's some lily sort of thing that I don't know the name of. Pink, I think, with this antenna doohickey sticking out…"

Geneva remembered Michael telling her he wanted to be kept informed of every detail, including the color of the flowers. He'd backed off on that a long time ago. If nothing else, at least he now trusted her to do her job.

"Geneva?"

"Hmm?" Chin on hand and staring into space, Geneva blinked. "I'm sorry. What?"

"The lilies?"

"Right." She sat up straight. "Just pick flowers you like. I've got a florist in mind and her work is genius. I was toying with the idea of a flower-decorated arbor where you and Dex will stand to take your vows."

Teri's eyes went dewy. "That sounds perfect."

It had been perfect, Geneva remembered, on the day she hadn't married Michael. Standing under an arbor of roses, hydrangeas and peonies, she'd explained to everyone that there would be no wedding. She'd proven herself in business, but personally? No strings attached meant no arbor, no flowers, no second chance.

No Michael.

"Geneva? Is something bothering you?"

"No. Of course not," she lied.

Why should it bother her that the last time she'd seen Michael she'd sensed a shift from distant to personal? Why should she be distracted because ever since then she'd been waiting for a sign that he cared?

Why should she be upset that she couldn't focus on anything but him? Why should—Oh, dear God. The official truth dawned on her.

Why? Because she'd fallen for Michael. Again.

"Not again," she murmured.

"What?" Teri frowned.

Technically she hadn't fallen in love with him again. Because she hadn't truly been in love the first time. She'd been infatuated. This was different— deeper, stronger, rooted in reality not fascination.

"Geneva, what's going on with you?"

She wasn't doing this again with Teri. "Nothing," she answered, nervously shuffling files.

Like dominoes, one cluttered pile pushed against the next until the papers on the far corner of her desk went over the side.

Teri bent to retrieve them, then frowned as she stared at one of the messages. "Does my brother know about this?"

"What?"

Geneva took the slip and read it. Events planner. Atlantic City. Offer you can't refuse. There was a company name, a contact and a phone number.

"Does Michael know you're looking for another job?" Teri's voice was tight with tension.

"I still have a contract." And she was pathetically grateful for it.

Geneva glanced at the slip of paper. "I have no idea what this is about, but I intend to find out."

"And when you do, are you going to talk to Michael?"

"This could be a complete waste of time. But if it's not, of course I'll talk to your brother."

Because a friend talked to a friend. This time around, while she'd been busy resisting him, Michael had become a friend. And so much more. This time she'd learned why he'd guarded his heart so carefully. When he'd given it to her, she'd been afraid to commit. Now she knew he was what she wanted for the rest of her life.

But she would only get the rest of the time left on her contract.

Geneva stood outside the door to Michael's office and took a deep breath. So much had happened since that day she'd pulled herself together in this very spot. The best thing was that she'd seen him naked again. The worst was that she'd fallen hopelessly in love.

As if everything wasn't complicated enough, now she had to make a career decision. Behind door number one: Stay put and hope she could show Michael that it could be different between them this time around. Door number two: Atlantic City and a big step up the success ladder. It was a good job offer or she'd have declined on the basis of her legal obligation to Michael. But she needed to know how he felt and his reaction to her leaving would tell her what she needed to know.

"Here goes," she whispered.

She knocked sharply once, then opened the door and walked in.

Michael looked up. "Hi."

"Hi, yourself."

"How are you?"

"Fine." She sat in one of the chairs facing his desk. Her legs were suddenly shaky and it had nothing to do with her employment future. Getting fired would be easy compared to this. Her entire future, her every happiness, was riding on the next few minutes.

"How are you?" she asked.

"Good."

"Are you really?"

She'd gotten to know him so well recently and instinct told her something was up. His eyes lacked the passion and spark she was used to when she was this close. There were lines in his face she hadn't seen before. He hadn't grinned the Michael Sullivan grin when he saw her.

"I'm great," he said.

"Is everything all right with Sullivan Towers? The financing is in place?"

"Things couldn't be better. Why?"

Because he'd put a lot of energy, man hours and money into this project and she wanted him to be wildly successful. The stress and pressure must be crushing and he was dealing with it alone.

Not the business part, of course. He had Dex and

the rest of his talented operations team. But he was the heart and soul of the project. With them he had to maintain the strong, self-confident, upbeat front. The buck stopped here in this office. Everyone got to dump on him.

But after hours, in that big palatial house of his, who did he dump on?

She'd only ever seen her parents pull each other apart. Michael had been the one to show her that shared burdens were easier to carry. She wanted to help him carry his.

"You look tired," she said.

"No." He leaned back in his chair. "Just focused."

"On?" she asked, giving him another opening.

"Work. The tower is sold out. Construction is set to start. Barring weather delays, building materials shortages, or any unforeseen setbacks, this high-rise is going to be everything I'd hoped."

"I'm glad to hear it, Michael."

And she was. Maybe it was being here in his office and the reminder of just how far they'd come, but the man before her was different from the Michael she'd come to know. He wasn't the man who'd held her while she cried in the back of his limo or the one who'd toasted his success with her in the moonlight.

"So what did you want to talk to me about?" Was there an edge to his voice? "You told my secretary there was something you needed to discuss."

"Right." She linked her fingers in her lap to hide

the fact that her hands were shaking. It was best to just spit it out. "I had a job offer."

Michael's expression didn't change. "I see."

"It's a really good career opportunity. Apparently Sullivan Towers wasn't the only beneficiary of all that publicity. Someone noticed my work and was impressed enough to contact me."

"I'm not surprised."

"That makes one of us. It came out of the blue for me."

"I don't know why. You're very good at what you do, Geneva. It was only a matter of time until someone snapped you up."

She wanted him to snap her up, and she waited for him to say something along those lines. She desperately needed to know how he felt about this, but his face was impassive.

What was that about? She'd never been president of a multimillion dollar corporation but if her assistant announced she had a job offer, Geneva would have questions. A lot of them. Off the top of her head she'd be asking who, what, when, where, why and how much were they paying so she could top it.

What would it take to get a rise out of Michael?

"It's in Atlantic City," she volunteered, wanting to point out the place was on the other side of the country. In case he needed a reminder. In case he cared that she'd be so far away.

"I'm glad you won't be working for one of my Vegas competitors."

So he knew his geography and wasn't fazed by the distance. Something pulled painfully tight in her chest. "I do have a contract with Sullivan, Inc., so maybe I should tell them to—"

"Not a problem. I can let you out of the agreement."

Please don't, she wanted to say. *Tell me I owe you. Tell me to stay.*

"If I'd known you were going to make this so difficult—" She was struggling to keep this light.

He shrugged. "This is what you want."

What she wanted was for him to say he loved her. Better yet, he should get mad and tell her not to go. Best of all, she'd like him to surge to his feet, block the door with the body that drove her crazy and ask her to stay because he couldn't live without her.

Instead what she was getting was him removing the speed bumps from her exit. She was hearing the message loud and clear. Don't let the door hit you on the way out. He'd been dead serious about no commitment.

"Then it's settled." It took every ounce of her self-control to hold off the pain until she could get out of his office. "Unless you have something else to say…"

"No."

"All right." She stood. "You'll have my resignation on your desk before I go home today."

He nodded. "Good luck, Geneva."

"Thanks."

With all her heart she wished to hear him say "I'll be in touch." But he didn't. He'd already focused his amazing powers of concentration on whatever work she'd interrupted.

She would never know how she made it to the door with her dignity intact. This was so much worse than the last time she'd left him because she'd learned how good they could be together. When she was alone, the tears she'd been holding back blurred her vision and trickled down her cheeks. Puffy eyes she could deal with. But she swore she could actually hear the sound of her heart breaking.

It was the last time Michael Sullivan would make her cry.

CHAPTER TWELVE

MICHAEL braced his elbows on his desk and rubbed his eyes. Letting out a long breath, he glanced at his watch, annoyed that it was only 9:00 p.m. He was tired, but not nearly tired enough. If he worked a little longer, maybe exhaustion would help him forget her.

Geneva.

She'd only left Las Vegas a week ago, but to him she was gone the moment Teri had told him about the job offer. Why was this so much worse than the last time she'd walked out on him?

Because he really knew her now.

Not just that she liked nuts in her chocolate. He realized she'd wanted their baby as much as he had and blamed herself for not being able to bring their child into the world. He'd known she was sassy and sexy in equal parts, but this time around he'd learned that she was bright and funny, too. And strong, yet so afraid of making a mistake that would turn the two of them into clones of her parents. If he'd known all that a year ago, he might not be sitting here now missing her. Wanting her. *Needing* her.

"Why in God's name are you still here?" Teri stood in his office doorway, hands on hips as she glared at him.

"Because I have work to do."

"Oh, please."

Michael leaned back in his chair, really not wanting to go into this. He felt raw. He felt Geneva's absence all the way to his soul.

"You look pretty," he said. Always nice when an attempt at distraction was also the honest truth. "Dinner with Dex?"

"We went to Pinnacle," she confirmed. "He's waiting downstairs. I had a feeling you'd still be in your office."

"Like I said, I've got work to do."

"You work too hard."

He shrugged. "I always hope the little business elves will sneak in overnight and get me caught up."

"It's not going to work, Michael."

"I know. The elves need a good talking to."

"That's not what I meant." Although the corners of her mouth curved up for a moment. "You can run, but you can't hide. I thought you'd stop her."

"Who?" It was a bluff.

"Don't play dumb. Why did you let Geneva go?"

"I had no right to stop her."

"What about the fact that you're in love with her?"

"I couldn't do that to her." He ran his fingers through his hair. "Think about it, Teri. Her parents used her to hurt each other and they did it in the name of love. She had a great career opportunity. If I'd told her how I felt, I'd just be one more person using love as a tool for personal gain. She needed to make her decision based on what's best for her," he insisted.

"And I'm concerned about what's best for you," Teri shot back. "Working until you're too tired to think? Hiding because someone made her an offer and she had the audacity to consider it—" She stopped and stared at him. "That's it."

"What?"

"I'm such an idiot." She huffed out a breath. "I just thought you should know she'd been approached by another company but as soon as I told you about her job offer, you disconnected. It was self-preservation."

He shifted and rested one elbow on the arm of his chair. Leave it to his sister to go for the jugular. This conversation was getting old. "How are the wedding plans coming along? You must be concerned about the details now."

"Geneva has it covered."

"Still, between now and then, you're on your own—"

"Stop, Michael. You're not getting off the hot seat by distracting me."

"From your amateur psycho babble—"

"I'm right and this time you're going to listen."

He shook his head. "You're not the boss of me."

Teri used to say that all the time when she was a little girl. She'd been shocked and grieving and he'd buried himself in college classes, work and taking care of her. Back then he *had* disconnected, to avoid dealing with his own shock and grief. And guilt, because he hadn't told his mother and father how much he loved them.

Teri's smile was tender. "You're not the only one who lost your parents. If anyone knows how you feel, it's me. But instead of trying not to care and avoid pain, knowing how fragile life is makes me more determined to grab onto happiness with both hands. Dex makes me happy and I want him in my life—with or without a binding legal contract."

"So you'd live in sin?"

"The biggest sin is turning your back on a chance for love. I'll admit it scares me. And I think it scares you, too."

"What's your point, Teri?"

"My point is that by not saying those all-important three words to Geneva, you guaranteed she would go. And you didn't have to take responsibility for your feelings."

He reined in his anger, then met his sister's gaze. "I tried to show her in every way possible how I feel about her."

"For the average woman that would be enough. But you and I both know that Geneva needs the words, too."

"Trust me, it was better that I didn't confuse the issue. She was free to decide what she wanted."

"That's the thing, Michael. You didn't give her all the facts for an informed decision. Remember what Dex's dad said at the engagement party? Life isn't measured by the breaths we take, but by the moments that take our breath away."

He remembered. And he remembered Geneva's words, too. His mother would be appalled that anything she'd said or done would negatively impact him. What if he *had* let her go because he was hiding? Looking for excuses to avoid telling her how he felt? He didn't like what that said about him.

"Are you finished, Teri? I need to get back to work so I can get home sometime tonight."

"You'd be there now if Geneva was waiting for you. You got a do-over, Michael, and you blew it."

That barb hit the mark and he barely suppressed a wince. But he kept his mouth shut because every time he said something, she turned it around on him.

"You make a fabulous living, but you have no life. If you let Geneva go again, you're an idiot." Teri stood and walked to the door. "*Now* I'm finished."

When he was alone, Michael went to the window and stared out at the lights on the Strip. Las Vegas was hyped as the most exciting city on the planet.

He'd always believed that, and he had worked hard to make Sullivan Towers the success it was turning out to be. But the triumph was empty without Geneva to share it.

He couldn't keep running on empty. He had to find a way to convince Geneva to come back to him. She was the only woman who could fill the void in his soul.

Geneva paced in her suite at the Atlantic City Resort, which was where she lived and worked now. The two bedroom, two bath luxury suite of rooms were hers for as long as she needed them. Cherry wood tables. Brass lamps. Comfortable bed. Lovely furniture. Elegant and sophisticated.

"It's nice," she said to herself.

She brushed aside the lace curtain covering the slider and glanced outside, sighing at the drab view. Not drab, she thought, struggling to be glass-is-half-full. It's just dark. In Las Vegas the neon lights glittered 24/7. It had the skyline, the view across the valley to the craggy mountains that surrounded it, the whole city was like nowhere else in the world. It was never dark.

"But Atlantic City has an ocean."

She would get used to her new address because one day would turn into the next. Comparisons between Atlantic City and Las Vegas would stop. She'd put one foot in front of the other and go to work every day, doing the best possible job. Everything strange would become familiar.

But would she ever get used to not seeing Michael?

Damn it. Michael Sullivan didn't want her. When she'd sat on the plane waiting to take off from McCarran Airport, she'd promised herself she wouldn't think about him.

"But I miss him," she said on a sigh.

With every fiber of her being.

That phrase had never been really clear to her until now. But the emptiness and pain inside touched her everywhere. He was the last person in her mind at night and the first person she thought about when she opened her eyes in the morning. She wondered if he was working too hard. If he was eating right and taking care of himself. If he missed her even a tiny bit.

"Enough."

Wallowing was pointless. Getting busy would take her mind off what she'd left behind. She walked into the bedroom, surveying the three open suitcases with clothes hanging out. She decided to work up some enthusiasm for unpacking. It was way past time to start nesting and snap out of her resistance to settling in.

A knock sounded at her door and she was grateful for the interruption that hopefully would postpone unpacking yet again. How pathetic was she?

"Who is it?" she called, standing in front of the door.

"Michael."

Her pulse jumped and she fumbled with the lock because her hands were trembling so badly. Finally she opened the door.

"Hello." She'd never know how she managed to form the word when her throat had gone dry.

She was afraid her imagination had produced him, and she couldn't look hard enough. His khaki pants and knit shirt were wrinkled. The five o'clock shadow gave him a reckless look that she had never seen before. The shadows beneath his eyes made her wonder if he'd slept in days. But it *was* him, and he was a sight for sore eyes. Or, more to the point, a sore heart.

"Are you...? Is everything all right?" she asked.

"Not really."

"What's wrong?"

"Can I come in?"

"Of course." She pulled the door wide, then closed it after him. "Is it Teri? Dex?"

His back was to her as he looked around. "Nice."

"Home away from—" She stopped. "It's very comfortable. Everyone has bent over backward to make me feel welcome and a part of the team."

He whirled, his face tight as he stared at her. "So you like it here?"

"So far... So-so."

She couldn't lie. She also couldn't stop shaking. And he hadn't answered her question. "Is everyone all right, Michael?"

"They're fine. They miss you. Chloe, the staff—" The muscle in his jaw jumped. "Everyone."

By definition, everyone included him. Or was that

just a pathetic attempt at hope? "How did you know where to find me?"

"Teri."

Of course. She'd made sure Teri knew how to get in touch because of the wedding. If her brain had been firing on all cylinders, she'd have realized that herself.

But there was only one question she really wanted the answer to and it was the one she was most afraid to ask. Except she wasn't the same woman who'd left him at the altar. If she'd learned anything it was that running away didn't solve the problem.

So she asked, "Why are you here, Michael?"

"I want you to come back." His voice was low, husky and threaded with raw desperation.

She took a step toward him, close enough to feel the heat of his body. "Why?"

"Because—This time—" He ran his fingers through his hair.

"What, Michael?"

His eyes glittered with something dark and dangerous. "Don't tell me it's too late."

She shook her head. "Too late for what?"

"When you told me about the job, I didn't want you to go," he said, not answering the question.

If only she'd known that's how he felt. "Why didn't you tell me?"

"I thought I was doing the right thing." He laughed, but the sound was bitter. "Hell of a time to find out that sometimes the right thing can be wrong.

I didn't want you to think I was using emotions against you."

"I understand. It's okay."

"No, it's not. That was just an excuse." He shook his head. "No more, Geneva. I've spent my life avoiding putting everything on the line."

"Define everything," she demanded.

"You." Intensity snapped in his dark eyes.

One word that changed everything. Still, there'd been so much hurt. "How can you feel like that? After what I did—"

He took her hands in his. "Forget the past. We start fresh. We start here. We have a future—if we can find the guts to take a chance. I haven't had a lot of practice with saying what's on my mind, but I'll do the best I can if you'll promise to listen with your heart."

"I promise." She held her breath.

"I need you, Geneva. Without you I have no life. I want children with you. I want to grow old with you. *I came after you.*"

Leave it to Michael. All she'd wanted was the three magic words, but he'd done her one better. If he'd scooped her into his arms and carried her up the curved staircase in a *Gone With the Wind* moment, she couldn't be more swept off her feet.

"Who says you're not good with words? Michael—" Happiness expanded inside her and squeezed her chest as she threw herself into his arms.

"I'm in love with you, Geneva." His shuddering breath stirred her hair.

"I love you, too," she said, holding him as tight as she could. "I love you so much."

"If we have a day, a week, a month, or a hundred years together, I want a chance to make breathless moments with you." He put her away from him, but didn't let her go. His gaze searched hers. "Geneva Porter, will you marry me?"

"Yes."

"Just like that?" he asked, a smile on his lips.

Not just like that. The answer had been more than a year in the making. From the bottom of her heart, she knew it was the right one.

A single tear slipped down her cheek. A tear that made her see more clearly. "I know what love feels like now, Michael. And we have the head-over-heels kind. The kind that makes a marriage work."

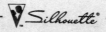

SPECIAL EDITION™

Experience the "magic" of falling in love at Halloween with a new *Holiday Hearts* story!

UNDER HIS SPELL

by KRISTIN HARDY

October 2006

Bad-boy ski racer J. J. Cooper can get any woman he wants—except Lainie Trask. Lainie's grown up with him and vows that nothing he says or does will change her mind. But J.J.'s got his eye on Lainie, and when he moves into her neighborhood and into her life, she finds herself falling under his spell....

THE
PART-TIME
WIFE

by *USA TODAY* bestselling author

Maureen Child

Abby Talbot was the belle of Eastwick society;
the perfect hostess and wife. If only her
husband were more attentiive. But when
she sets out to teach him a lesson and files
for divorce, Abby quickly learns her husband's
true identity...and exposes them to scandals
and drama galore!

On sale October 2006 from Silhouette Desire!

Available wherever books are sold,
including most bookstores, supermarkets,
discount stores and drug stores.

I N T I M A T E   M O M E N T S™

CAN THREE ALPHA WARRIORS WITH A BLOOD-BOND AND NO PASTS CHANGE THE SHAPE OF THE WORLD'S FUTURE?

Find out in Intimate Moments' new trilogy filled with adventure, betrayal and passion by

LORETH ANNE WHITE

THE HEART OF A MERCENARY
October 2006, #1438

A SULTAN'S RANSOM
November 2006, #1442

RULES OF REENGAGEMENT
December 2006, #1446

AVAILABLE WHEREVER YOU BUY BOOKS.
